ALSO BY STEPHANIE MIRRO

THE LAST PHOENIX
Wings of Fire
Wings of Death
Wings of Winter
Wings of Magic
Wings of Life
Wings of Deceit
Wings of Mercy

IMMORTAL RELICS
Curse of the Vampire
Fury of the Gods
Revenge of the Witch
Rise of the Demons

COLLECTIONS
The Outsiders: An Hourlings Anthology

Dedication

For Marty, who always pushes for more boobs, blood, and badassery. This series is even better because of your keen eye and (extremely) candid feedback.

WINGS OF MAGIC

THE LAST PHOENIX: BOOK FOUR

STEPHANIE MIRRO

TANNHAUSER PRESS

Visit stephaniemirro.com for more information

Cover design by Luminescence Covers
Published by Tannhauser Press
tannhauserpress.com

Print ISBN: 978-1-945994-64-7

May 2021

10 9 8 7 6 5 4 3 2 1

CHAPTER 1

Friday at Dawn

Traveling through portals was not made for the phoenix kind. How did I know this? Because so far, I was two-for-two when it came to traversing a frigid plane of nothingness while shivering my tits off. Scientists might not consider two trips a reasonable number to base a statistically sound judgment, but I wasn't a fucking scientist.

No, I was a walking Veronica popsicle and quite possibly lost in between realms.

The last time, on my way to the fae realm known as the Otherworld, it hadn't taken nearly as long. But I had no idea where I was headed this time, or even if some dimensions were farther than others. For all I knew, I could be headed straight for hell. That kind of heat sounded fucking fantastic right about now.

My whole body shook, my teeth a clattering mess that, besides my shuffling feet, was the only sound in this desolate wasteland. I stumbled onward through the never-ending grey mist, rubbing my hands together and blowing into them as if it would somehow help. My inner fire—as in the source of my magic, not my spirited nature—had only partly returned, and I refused to use it unless I froze in place. It was too precious to waste. But also, what good would it do if I was truly lost?

Had I known I'd be realm-jumping today, I would have prepared by dressing smart, like wearing a jacket for starters. Too bad I'd dressed for a fight in hot and humid Miami. The bite on my calf burned beneath the rip in my pants, which probably wasn't a good sign but was the least of my concerns right now. It was the only warm part of my body. I almost longed for it to spread, but I wasn't that desperate…

Yet.

What kind of idiot goes running into a portal without even knowing where she would end up? Oh, that's right— *me.* I followed William and his necromancer wannabes because he dared to take away my new friend and the only other phoenix I had met outside my family. I even left the man I love behind.

Thane.

His name froze on my lips. I fell to my knees and curled into myself, my lungs constricting, making it hard to catch a breath. Had a breeze swept by and made it even colder? Was that even possible here, wherever here was?

Damn it all to hell. I couldn't think about leaving him

right now, or about the devastated look on his beautiful face when he realized what I was about to do. And if my thoughts swerved to my best friend Kit and how she almost killed me in her grief-turned-rage, I would be done for. I would just lie down right here and never move again.

Nope, not going there. I had to help Ivan. It was my fault William captured him instead of me, with the monstrous goal of harnessing Ivan's phoenix magic to raise whole battlefields of the dead.

I leaned forward on my hands and knees and crawled, not yet willing to give in to the possibility of being stuck in between worlds. I sure as hell wasn't ready to consider never seeing Thane again, especially not thanks to my foolishness.

Raw and red, my fingers ached as I clutched at the ground and pulled myself forward. I couldn't even feel the grass beneath my hands anymore—

Wait.

Grass?

Everything around me was a shaky blur as my entire body shivered, but I wasn't in a frozen tundra anymore. Dawn lit up the sky with widely spread golden tendrils, allowing more than enough light to see my surroundings. Leaf-filled and flowering trees reached toward the sky, explosions of color everywhere I turned. Dried seeds and pods littered the clearing around me, as did patches of vibrant green grass from where the sun peeked through the thick branches above.

I was in a forest.

Holy shit. I'd made it through the never-ending portal. I crumbled all the way to the ground in relief, happiness, and exhaustion. A sob escaped my lips, and I allowed my inner flame to warm me at last. I lay on my side and closed my eyes, ready to let the darkness take me while the heat defrosted my body.

Metal clashing against metal hit my ears like a thunderclap. I sat up, somehow instantly alert. The unmistakable sounds of fighting with steel made their way through the trees, along with grunts and yells as people took hits or gave them.

Ivan.

With the phoenix's name on my numb lips, which I was sure were cracked and blue, I scrambled to my feet and ran toward the clangs of battle. Adrenaline could do some crazy shit to get a body moving again, but I would pay for it later. That was a problem for future Veronica.

I ducked beneath low branches, twigs, and leaves crunching beneath my feet. A weird squirrel-like animal with long ears and two tails stared at me from its perch to my right, but I didn't have time to stop and figure it out.

Ivan needed me.

I burst out of the trees and onto a dirt road. Sure enough, scuffles had broken out between the necromancer mages I'd followed from the human world and some newcomers. It was easy to tell the mages from the others since William's idiots all dressed in ridiculous floor-length black robes and carried staffs. At this point, anyone fighting against the maniacal fae necromancer and his minions was an immediate friend of mine.

Without another thought, I drew two of my knives and threw myself at one of the black-robed mages. I was lucky to still have the blades, having the foresight to tuck them back into their sheaths right after entering the portal. If I hadn't, chances were I would have lost them in the world between, falling from my frozen fingers.

The mage blocked my attack with his staff. I nearly lost my footing when my knee threatened to give. The werewolf bite on my leg screamed in pain. I had to ignore it for now, though, and hope someone here had some Advil or something until my magic replenished enough to burn out the infection.

Amputation might do the trick, too.

I sliced the mage across the arm. The quick-acting sleeping poison coated on my blade immediately took hold. He crumpled to the side. I met one of the newcomers' gazes—a tall guy, slim, with bright blond hair and a cheeky, dimpled grin. He winked sangria-hued eyes at me, an eye color I'd never seen before. My eyebrows raised in surprise, then we both had to duck under swings.

Between jabs, I realized William and Ivan weren't even here, and I was pretty sure they hadn't been when I jumped into the fight. I wanted to scream a line of expletives into the air, but my vision went swirly for a moment, distracting me. I wiped the sweat from my forehead before it dripped into my eyes.

The last of the mages fell with a sword through his middle, courtesy of one of the new guys. I preferred not to kill unless I had no other choice—something that had become more common in recent days—but I didn't judge others for doing so. Especially not when it came to the necromancers.

I panted and bent over with both hands on my knees as I looked around the area. The newcomers were wiping off blades and securing the few mages who survived.

"Where are the other mages?" I asked. "The Winter Court fae?"

The tall guy who winked at me earlier frowned at me now, suspicion narrowing his strange, purplish-red eyes. Like Ivan had been, this man was dressed in leather clothing, only he also wore thick shoulder pauldrons and brandished a longsword. He gripped the sword's pommel tighter as he looked me up and down.

"You're not human." His voice held the slightest hint of an accent I couldn't place.

As a wave of nausea swept through me, I sheathed my knives. In part, a display of good faith that I wasn't the enemy, but also because it would really suck to land on one of my own blades if I fell over. The sun's light was blinding now, and I squinted up at him, catching the hint of otherness about him and his friends now that the fight wasn't distracting me.

"No shit, Sherlock. Neither are you."

"Then why are you speaking in a human tongue?" he asked.

I noticed that the group of newcomers had me surrounded—five of them, fully armed and dressed in the same type of leather armor. And only one of me in cargo pants and a tank top and most definitely not at my best. Fuck. "And what other tongue would you expect me to speak?"

"*Yazyk.* That of the *feniks.*" He swept his arm toward the others. "You're one of us."

My mouth dropped open, and I tried to tilt my head to the side, except I ended up falling to my knees as my whole world spun with the head movement. "Is this *Mirognya?*"

"Of course. Are you friend or foe to the crown?" The others closed in as he questioned me.

"I… I have no idea." I licked my dry lips. "I came through a portal following the mages. They took my friend. He's a phoenix. A feniks." Forming words was getting a bit difficult, like my tongue was swelling up. I hoped it wasn't, though, or else I might end up swallowing it. I took a deep breath. "He said his name was Ivan."

The phoenix's name sent a flurry of whispers and furtive glances among them. One of the others stepped forward and knelt in front of me. A woman. She had long black hair worn in dreadlocks but secured away from her cheeks with some sort of leather tie. The olive-toned skin of her face had been covered beneath some swirly purple tribal makeup—a warrior woman. The rest of her was kind of blurry.

"You're a friend of Ivan's?" she asked.

I attempted to smile, but my cheeks felt a bit sluggish. "I think so. He reminds me of my brother, Maddox." I fell over, my chest heaving as I struggled to get enough air.

"What's wrong with you?" she asked, her eyebrows furrowed.

"Bite on my leg. Werewolf… I think… infected…"

The world went dark.

CHAPTER 2

Unknown Day

Days and nights, weeks, or even months could have passed for all I knew. I woke from time to time, emerging from a fitful sleep and crying out for water as the fever threatened to consume me. Someone changed and pressed cold compresses to my forehead and chest in an attempt to keep my temperature down. It didn't seem to be working, but I wasn't known for my patience with these types of situations. Make that in most situations.

In my more lucid moments, I knew that I didn't want to become a werewolf. Nothing about their pack-driven, alpha-lead lifestyle appealed to me in the slightest, and I made sure to tell anyone who might be listening.

Wild wolves didn't even follow an alpha the way werewolves did. That need for domination came from human genetics. I thought I cauterized my wound well enough before leaving the human world, but I hadn't even known if cauterizing it would stop the spread. Clearly my body was telling me otherwise.

Besides not wanting to wolf-out, I was terrified.

Not of dying, of course, because I would just resurrect. Maybe that would even fix the problem.

No, I was scared that the infection might somehow affect my phoenix abilities. With my limited knowledge, I'd never heard of a phoenix being infected. Would I even be able to shift into a falcon anymore? It might sound vain or downright ridiculous, but being a phoenix was my identity. With my family gone, it was all I had left. Even Kit had moved on.

Unfortunately, I didn't have too many lucid moments to worry about those things.

The rest of the time, I lived in a nightmare.

Visions of my past and possible futures haunted me, showing me what could have been or never would be or even what might be based on my failures in life. Maddox's limp hand on the side of the bed while Jackson Reed stood over him, grinning, his hands coated in blood. There hadn't been any real blood involved in Mad's death, but the image of that monster so close to my baby brother chilled me to the bone.

Thane came next, his accusing gaze speaking loud enough for him because he never spoke in my dreams. He only looked from Maddox to me, accusing me with his soulful, ocean-blue eyes. But he knew how hard I tried to get answers. Why the hell was he blaming *me?*

Because I didn't try hard enough when Mad was alive, that's why. Guilt gripped everything inside of me, twisting and pulling painfully. Thane turned and walked away, ignoring my pleas to stop.

Something cold touched my forehead, and I groaned. It felt glorious and awful at the same time.

"The fever's broken," said a woman to my right. I didn't recognize the higher-pitched, lilting voice, but my eyelids were too heavy to lift to find out who she was.

"How much longer until she wakes?" asked another unfamiliar voice, male this time. Deep and commanding, sending a sliver of apprehension up my back. Either of them could kill me right now, and I wouldn't be able to do a damn thing about it.

Where the hell was I?

My mouth wouldn't obey my commands to open—all my limbs and muscles felt too weary of doing anything but rest, which they did fantastically well, much to my dismay.

"Unknown," said the woman. Warm hands moved the sheet up my body and tucked it in around my shoulders. The creak of a chair and swish of fabric rubbing together, two sets of nearly silent footsteps moving away, the click of a door shutting, then silence.

I was alone, without a clue as to where I was or who these people were. More importantly, I wasn't a werewolf. At least, I didn't think so. I sure didn't feel like one. Did that mean I had to wait for a full moon?

Sweet Mokosh, I wish I had paid attention to my lessons better. I was sure my parents had gone over the process of turning into a werewolf once or twice, but my stubborn brain refused to dredge that information up.

I knew wolves could shift forms at any time like me, but I had an inkling of memory telling me the change only completed itself at a full moon. Technically, an undead werewolf bit my leg. Perhaps a Risen wolf bite didn't do anything except hurt and make the wound infected from common bacteria. As in from a mouth that's been decaying below ground for who knows how long before chomping into people's skin. Gross. Godsdamn William and his world domination via zombie plan.

Oh well. I guess I would find out whether I'd be howling at the moon soon enough. Back to the matter at hand.

Who the fuck were these people?

My finger twitched. Ognebog's flames! I could move.

I pulled on my inner fire, which was swirling around inside me, happily replenished and giddy to be used. I sent the flame all around my body, giving myself a boost of energy. Being a phoenix meant my wounds healed faster than a human, but my magic was mostly about destruction and complete rebirth. It wouldn't help much now, but it would allow me a small window of time to check the place out before I passed out again.

With great effort, I peeled my eyelids open. A haze filled my vision. I blinked a few times to clear it, then focused on what was right above me—a ceiling. I was inside somewhere. Good to know.

Without turning my head in case someone I hadn't heard or sensed was still in the room, I made out a wall on my left. Smooth grey stone of some sort, just like the ceiling. I couldn't see any windows for a potential escape yet, but the room's darkness suggested it was nighttime.

I turned my head a fraction of an inch to the right—the room was empty. I sighed in relief. Now I could snoop better.

The windowless, wooden door stood on the far wall, some kind of metal water pump with a small basin attached took up a corner to the door's left. A few blue-leafed plants hung from the ceiling in decorative planters. Flame-shaped sconces decorated the walls, but only two near the door had been turned on and at a low setting.

A wooden chair stood close to my bed, and I spied a cup of what I hoped was water. I licked my dry, cracked lips, very aware of how thirsty I was, but my limbs were too heavy from exhaustion to lift. Urging the little bit of energy I had into my arm, I lifted the limb toward the chair. Excitement rippled through me, giving me another boost to reach for the cup. Almost there…

My arm dropped, exhaustion winning over once again.

Fuck.

The door opened, and a woman with a long swishy skirt slipped inside. She closed the door and walked toward me, holding a tray. I couldn't make out the details of her shadowy features because the light was behind her.

"Oh, good, I was right." A hint of sarcasm tinted her otherwise warm and inviting voice. "I had a feeling you'd woken."

"Where am I?" I croaked.

She placed the tray on a small table near my head. I didn't even see the table before, but it was far closer than the chair and held another cup I could have easily reached.

Motherfucker.

She picked up the cup and held it to my lips. "You're safe, that's where."

I let her help me drink because my body returned to not moving again. The water's coolness soothed my parched and aching throat. Sleep was already tugging at my brain, but I had too many questions to let it rest just yet.

She set the cup down and flicked her wrist. A light above the table grew to life as if on a dimming switch, allowing me to see her better. Her long hair was black, quite possibly the same shade of midnight as Thane's, and shiny like satin. She'd done it in several thick braids before twisting them artfully around her head. Her eyes were a super light blue, and her skin had more of an olive tone than the man I met in the forest.

The forest.

Phoenixes.

Holy shit.

"I need to find Ivan," I said, my voice still rough but not as frog-like. "The fae mage who kidnapped him wants to harness his magic."

"We already have people searching for them," she said.

"Did you guys question the captured mages?" I asked, struggling to sit up only to find my muscles too weak to respond.

She rested a hand on my shoulder. "You need to rest. We have things under control."

I succumbed to the annoying inability to move. "Are you a phoenix, too?"

"We all are." She tilted her head to the side. "But I've been told you're from the human realm."

"Yes."

She lifted a bowl from the tray, stirred the contents with a spoon, then lifted the spoon to my mouth. I accepted it because I needed whatever nourishment I could get right now. There were far easier ways to kill someone than to feed them poison, like stabbing them. Less messy, though.

Oh well.

I swallowed the salty liquid—bone broth. Perfect.

"You're in Mirognya. Well, *Mirfeniksa*, to be exact. The realm of the *feniksy*." She continued to feed me. "I'm Lizabeta, but most people just call me Liz."

Mirognya. My stomach did a little flip-flop. When I first heard the word in the fae woods during my meeting with the stag—known as the Keeper of the Forest—I didn't know what it meant. Now I knew it was the phoenix realm, and I was actually there. Here. I had made it to the world my parents left. Maybe I'd finally find out why they never came back.

I swallowed before attempting a smile. "I'm Veronica, usually called V."

"Welcome to our home, V." Tiny crinkles formed beside her eyes when she smiled. "We're in—"

The door slammed open behind us, sending a rain of dust and pebbles down from the ceiling. Liz jumped and spilled soup onto her lap. Letting out a tirade of words in another language at whoever had just entered, she attempted to mop up the liquid before it soaked into her skirt. She blocked my view of whoever had caused such a mess.

"Enough," said the man's deep voice from earlier, cutting Liz off and sending goosebumps up my arms. Heavy footsteps strode closer until he was visible.

He was tall, *real* tall, his head almost brushing the ceiling. If I had to guess, I'd say he was 6'4", if not taller. White-blond hair—like mine when it wasn't dyed this awful brown—fell straight to brush against his shoulders, but his skin was several shades darker than mine. Naturally rich brown rather than tanned. An equally blond beard hugged his chin, but strands of black and red mixed together to darken it in mesmerizing patterns.

He wasn't just tall, either. He was *big*. His chest was broad, and defined muscles twitched beneath the white shirt he wore as he closed in on the bed.

And his eyes? His eyes were breathtaking—a mix of blues, greens, and even purple. Despite the rainbow, they were hard and fierce as he glared down at me.

He leaned closer, a hand resting purposefully on a sword's hilt at his side. "Who sent you?"

CHAPTER 3

Unknown Day

From my place on the bed, I squinted up at the giant of a man, bristling at the insinuation that I was doing someone else's dirty work. I did my own, thank you very much. "First of all, nobody *sends* me anywhere. Second, how fucking tall *are* you?"

Faster than I could blink, the man's large hand was around my throat, rough calluses scratching my skin. He clenched a dagger in his other, held where I could see it, though noticeably not at my throat. He didn't want to hurt me, but he wanted answers. The sharp steel glinted in the light. "Who sent you?"

I coughed as he squeezed. It didn't hurt, just enough

pressure to be an annoyance.

Liz placed a small yet firm hand on his arm. "I hardly think this tactic is necessary. She was answering my questions just fine until you came bursting in like a griffin in a pottery shop."

The sass was strong with that one. I liked her.

He let some of the pressure off my throat but didn't let go. "I will not ask you a fourth time. Who sent you?"

I swallowed, trying to wet my still-parched mouth and throat. "You could ask me ten more times, and the answer would be the same. No one sent me. I followed a crazy-ass fae mage into a portal he opened because he took my new friend."

"And you claim Ivan to be that friend?" he asked.

"Yeah. To be fair, we had only just met, but he'd been stalking me for weeks."

After a few seconds stare showdown, the man released me and moved back. I wanted to sit up and give him a piece of my mind for treating me so poorly, but I didn't have the strength. Damn undead werewolf.

"Tell me who you are," he said. Well, demanded. This guy didn't seem to be doing much else. If I had any energy, I would totally play with that, take a walk on the wild side and see how far I could push him.

"As I've already told your friend, I'm V." If he was going to ask vague questions, I would give him vague answers. Okay, I guess I could still play a little bit.

He stared at me, clearly waiting for more, so I just stared right back. Take that, asshole.

"And V stands for…?" he finally caved.

"Veronica."

"Veronica, what?"

"Neill."

The lines along his jaw moved as he grit his teeth. "How did you meet Ivan?"

"He was following me like a total creep show," I said, "and when I finally caught up to him, he told me who he was."

The man and Liz exchanged a glance.

"What exactly did he tell you?" he asked.

"That his name was Ivan, and he was looking for something."

He gestured for me to continue. "And?"

I tried to glare up at him, but my eyelids were too heavy for it to be effective. "And that's it. Like I said, we had just met. Speaking of which, who the hell are *you*?"

He sheathed his dagger; I must have passed some test. He said something to Liz in their other language, then he left, shutting the door a little softer than when he had burst in.

"What was all that?" I asked, my voice getting raspier from use and abuse.

"*That* was Pietr." She rolled her eyes. "He's not always that obnoxious, but he's been on edge lately." She got up and moved to the water pump, using the lever to fill a cup. When she returned to the bedside, she helped me drink again. It was blissfully cool and refreshing.

Speaking of the obnoxious devil, Pietr could have gotten quite the show. The sheet covering me slipped down during my encounter with the man. Someone must have changed my clothes because I was in some sort of long nightgown. I didn't even want to know who had seen me naked this time. I had passed out more than once in front of Thane and Kit. Even Jessa. Now, these new people.

Why was this becoming a thing in my life?

"Is Pietr your boss?" I asked after a few sips.

"You could say that." She set down the cup and picked up the soup bowl. "This has cooled quite a bit, but it'll still give you nourishment to regain your strength."

I let her feed me a few spoonfuls. When she sat back again, I asked, "Where are we exactly? And why is Pietr so demanding about my intentions? Who are you people?"

"You're in *Gavan*, which means Haven in your tongue," she explained. "Pietr created it as a refuge for those of us fleeing the capital."

I frowned. "Why did you flee? And what do you mean by 'it'? Created what exactly?"

Her smile was sad this time. "All of that can come later."

Sleep beckoned to me like a lover, caressing my limbs and drawing me down into its depths faster than before. "Did you drug me?"

"What your body and flame need most right now is rest." She set the empty bowl on the tray.

"So, you drugged me." My words were getting sluggish and sloppy.

"I'm putting you back into a medically-induced sleep, which means yes, I drugged you." She patted my arm. "Nighty night."

The next day—or maybe even longer for all I knew in this windowless room—I held onto the cool, stone wall for support as I finished taking shaky steps around the room. Thirty-nine steps all the way around, and this was my fourth such lap. My legs threatened to buckle, but I wasn't sure I'd be able to get back up if I fell.

"Good, we'll do more after lunch," Liz said, pointing to the bed.

I didn't need any more encouragement. Letting out a sigh, I collapsed onto the twin-sized bed and leaned against the wall for support.

Before my brief wake-up to meet Liz and Pietr, I'd slept for almost four days straight. Most of it was medically induced, but four days was apparently enough to make my whole body go soft. And here I thought almost getting eaten alive by a nest of vampires took a long time to recover from, but that had only taken two days.

Although to be fair, my pseudo guardian angel healed me that time. If Jessa were here, maybe it would have taken half the time to recover from this bite, too.

I bit my lip, not wanting to dwell too much on everything and everyone I missed from home. I needed to get back and make sure Thane and Kit were okay. Thinking of them and how we had left things made my heart clench painfully. I wanted to kick myself for not thinking my rash decision through. Impulsivity sucked sometimes.

Healing methods aside, an infection from an undead werewolf was no joke. I still didn't know if a bite from a living wolf would be more intense and therefore harder to reject, even with an angel's healing. The good news was I hadn't turned into a wolf.

The room I'd been staying in was inside a cave. I didn't know much else yet, like how far below ground we were because Liz refused to tell me anything more. I wasn't quite a prisoner; more like a diplomatic guest who was treated with an abundance of caution in case I turned out to be a spy. For whom or what, I still didn't know, but I definitely planned to find out.

The only thing she would tell me was that they were still looking for Ivan and the mages, and no, I wasn't allowed to help.

Like they could stop me if I tried.

"How long have you lived in Haven?" I accepted the cup of water Liz handed to me, thankful that I could drink it on my own now.

"A few years." Someone knocked at the door, and she rose to answer it. I couldn't see who was on the other side, but the person passed Liz a tray. A mouthwatering scent drifted toward me, and my stomach growled in response.

Chuckling, she set the tray down on the bedside table and retook her seat. "Perfect timing for breakfast. This is a bit more substantial than the soup from yesterday."

Okay, so I was right that it had only been a day since my interrogation at knife-point. One question answered, so many more to go.

I put my cup on the table and took the bowl. Chicken noodle soup—that's what it looked like, anyway. Whatever it was, I was ravenous. I held the bowl close to my mouth, relieved I no longer needed to be fed like a baby bird, and shoveled the noodles inside.

Sweet Mokosh's embrace. I might have even groaned a little bit.

Liz laughed. "I'm glad you approve of our meager offerings. We don't eat nearly as well as those in *Sokol*, the capital." Her face darkened with her last words.

I swallowed what I had in my mouth. "What was so bad that made you leave?"

"Here in Mirfeniksa, we follow a matriarchal style of government," Liz said, carefully choosing her words. "Our *tsarina*, like a queen to the humans, has ruled for nearly three decades, but some of us do not agree with her goals and methods for achieving them."

"Like what?" I asked.

"Now's not the time to get into politics, but Pietr led some of us to Haven to start our own community with our own rules."

"In secret, not sanctioned by the tsarina," I deduced.

She smiled. "Yes."

"Well, you're in luck. I happen to love rebels and renegades." I shoved another spoonful of noodles into my mouth.

"I had a feeling that would be the case," she said, giving me a knowing smile.

When I finished the soup, I set the bowl on the tray. My eyelids and limbs drooped, too heavy to lift. "Did you drug me again?"

"Nope. Your body just needs rest, and you need to listen to it." She helped me lay down and pulled the sheet up over me. "Sleep now, V."

And I did.

Once again, Liz came back into the room just as I opened my eyes. Or maybe she was there the entire time and only stepped out for a moment. I was out like a broken lightbulb as soon as I laid down, so who knew.

Either way, she brought me lunch—more noodle soup, which I devoured just as quickly as the first time—then told me the best news: I was allowed to leave the room. I jumped at the chance.

Just, not literally.

"You sure you don't want to hold on to me?" Liz asked, one eyebrow raised. Her look of disbelief in my ability to walk was enough to fuel my need to prove her wrong.

"I got this." I shooed away her attempt to help me.

Sometimes all it took was a little positive self-talk and an overabundance of stubbornness to be right. I let go of the room's stone wall and stood on quivering legs. Only a few hours had passed since my last excursion around my room, but it was time to get these puppies moving again. Plus, I was itching to check out more of this place.

Liz held the wooden door open as I made my way toward her. I was definitely the turtle in this race. Step by agonizingly slow step, I made my way out into the corridor beyond the room.

We were still in the cave, at the end of a long, rounded tunnel. Arched wooden doors like the one we'd come from spanned the length of it. The hallway curved six doors down, making it impossible to see where it ended, but the air was as warm here as it was in my room. A variety of scents teased my nose, everything from a rich, earthy smell to something like cinnamon or brown sugar.

A man stood waiting for us, his thumbs tucked casually

under his belt. I did a double-take when I recognized him.

His golden blond hair was hard to miss even in the dim light, but the dark red hue of his eyes looked blacker without the sunlight blinding me. He was tall and slim but far from weak. Lean muscles shifted beneath his tanned skin as he moved away from the wall. Like before, he wore a leather getup consisting of a brown tunic and pants.

"I've met you," I said lamely, wishing I'd thought to ask Liz for names.

Not that there had been any doubt, but his cheeky grin confirmed it. The man had some seriously cute dimples. "I'm Pavel. Good to see you standing again, stranger."

I smiled. "I'm V, and I'm glad I'm not a wolf, thanks to all of you."

His grin turned devious. "Has enough time passed to be sure?"

Well, shit. "Honestly, I have no idea."

"Stop heckling her." Liz tsked. "You'll be fine."

He held up his hands in surrender. "We don't have were-things here, but they sound fascinating from what I've read."

"Do you guys have any other types of species here?" My legs wobbled slightly, and I reached out to the wall to steady myself. "On two feet, I mean."

"Let's walk and talk," Liz said before he could answer.

Pavel swept an arm out and led the way.

With Liz at my side watching me like a mother hen, I followed him down the hallway, stumbling from time to time on the rough stone floor. I didn't have shoes on anymore, and the coolness seeped through the soles of my feet. On an average day, the temperature would make me wish for shoes.

Today, I reveled in the feeling, knowing it meant I was on my own two feet and walking without Liz's help, even if I had to keep waving her away. Besides, it wasn't freezing, just slightly cooler than the cave's dense humidity.

My gaze wandered over the shape of the walls and rounded ceiling, only a foot higher than Pavel's head and smooth besides the bits of moss and roots poking through. I wondered what kind of tools had shaped these tunnels so perfectly for phoenix use. How far down into the ground were we? And why did they keep their guest quarters—or prisoner cell blocks, whatever I was considered right now—underground?

"We have some creatures that I don't think exist in the human realm," Pavel answered my question as we walked. "Like griffins and unicorns."

I stopped so suddenly I almost fell over. "Wait, there are unicorns here? Legitimate unicorns?"

Pavel turned to grin at me. "Oh yes, and they're just as feisty as you'd think."

I didn't actually think of unicorns as feisty at all. The fairytales I read as a kid described them as calm, majestic creatures who only showed themselves to virgin girls or some bullshit like that.

"They're difficult to catch and tame, so they remain mostly in the wild," he continued when I regained enough composure to keep shuffling along. "But the griffins work for us. They're exceptionally strong, so they carry people and goods around Mirfeniksa when we can't fly them ourselves."

"Instead of taxis and airplanes?" I asked.

Pavel glanced at me curiously. "I know what a taxi is, but what are airplanes?"

"Big taxis that can fly," I explained, realizing how difficult it was to explain things I'd taken for granted. "Like a giant, metal bird."

He nodded. "Sounds about the same then."

What an odd concept. Just how big were these beasts?

Before I had a chance to wonder further or ask more about this new realm, we made a sharp right. The hallway opened into an expansive cavern the size of a high school football stadium and several stories tall. My eyebrows shot to my hairline as I took in the scene below us.

It wasn't just a cavern, I realized—it was a whole town.

We stood at the top of a stone staircase carved from the wall, leading down into the heart of it all. Similar stairs and darkened hallways leading deeper into the earth dotted the walls all around us. At the bottom, various activities were happening simultaneously, illuminated by sconces along the walls and eclectic light fixtures throughout.

Farthest from where we stood, three people hustled and bustled in a kitchen, serving food to those waiting in line— the lunch crowd. After collecting their meal, the patrons would take their trays to a handful of tables and chairs set up nearby.

Next to the kitchen was a small food market, with buckets and barrels filled with fresh produce. I assumed they were fruits and veggies, at any rate. I squinted, trying to make out any recognizable shapes. Most of it didn't look like any plants I had ever seen. Not that I ever claimed to be a botanist.

Directly below us was a group of people sitting in a circle, their hands moving almost too fast for me to follow. They were weaving and sewing, creating clothing that hung on racks nearby. Kids ran through the entire area, laughing and yelling and adding to the general chaos. I smiled. Such was their right.

By my side, Liz said, "Welcome to Haven."

CHAPTER 4

Tuesday Afternoon

Something seemed off about the scenes below until realization smacked me over the head like a frying pan, an experience I was oddly familiar with. There were no cell phones in this common area, no computers, no sewing machines, not even modern clothing, or a cash register at the market.

There was a distinct sense of old-world living with everything here, like technology didn't reach inside the cave, so they had to make do without. For all I knew, it could be like this everywhere in Mirognya, which was strange considering they had access to the human world. Ivan was proof of that.

But the fact that they made their own clothes and served food inside a cave made me question just how unsafe it was for them outside. What could be so bad that they'd hide this way, and for how long?

What kind of monsters existed up above?

"Where do the other tunnels go?" I asked, lifting my gaze to the other stairs, then up to the sloping roof at least another two stories above us. Several gaps spotted the ceiling, presumably opening to the world above.

Falcons of various sizes and colors came and went through the holes. Those flying in descended and shifted on stair platforms or the floor, waving to friends or going about their business.

"To other homes and baths and the like," Liz said, though her answer sounded a bit short, like she was holding something back.

"I didn't realize your whole town was down here," I said. "How many of you live here?"

Liz glanced at Pavel before answering, "A few hundred."

I didn't blame them for the hesitation and vague answers; they didn't know me. And from what I'd learned so far, they had a more significant reason for being so cautious. Who knew what the tsarina would do to defectors?

I wanted to go down and explore, to meet people and ask them all about their lives, but Liz stopped me when I took a step in that direction.

"Baby steps," she said with a laugh. "You might make it down if you're lucky, but you won't make it back up on those shaky legs. Besides, you're still in a nightgown."

I looked down at the long shirt covering my body

before opening my mouth to protest, but she shook her head. "Neither of us is going to carry you, and I doubt even your falcon would have enough energy. Pietr has also forbidden mingling or flying just yet."

Well, that explained it.

I snapped my mouth shut and glared at the two phoenixes who simply regarded me with amusement. "I know we've just met and all, but I'm not exactly good at following the rules."

Paval grinned. "You don't say."

"Lucky for you, I am." Liz led me by the arm back toward the hallway. "He'll grant you access eventually, but for now, you still need to rest."

I grumbled but let her lead me along. As much as I hated to admit it—which was a lot—my legs felt like Jell-O after the brief walk down the hall. I couldn't imagine how exhausted I'd be after a few flights of stairs. The stubborn side of me wanted to prove everyone wrong, myself included. So I was silently grateful to have someone telling me no, a fact I'd never admit to anyone.

Once again, we passed by the other doors along the corridor. One opened a few feet ahead of us, and a woman stepped out, her bright red hair streaked with silver. Besides her hair, only a few wrinkles beside her eyes and mouth gave away her advancing age. As in a few hundred years old. I knew from my parents that even phoenixes didn't escape all the signs of old age.

Sharp brown eyes swept across the three of us, widening when they settled on me. Her mouth parted slightly, and she took a step back.

"Are you okay, Mama Anya?" Liz asked in English. I

assumed for my benefit.

Mama Anya shook her head as if to clear her thoughts and composed herself. She and Liz spoke quickly in the phoenix language, gesturing at me like I wasn't standing right there. Satisfied with whatever Liz explained, the woman gave me a curt nod before leaving us.

"What was that about?" I asked, following her departing back with my gaze. Her reaction left me unsettled, and I rubbed at the goosebumps crawling up my arm.

Liz rolled her eyes. "She thought you looked familiar, but I told her that was impossible unless she'd gone to the human realm in the last few decades."

Pavel grinned. "Mama Anya is suspicious of all newcomers."

"With good reason." Liz gave him a pointed look then nudged me onward again.

"You've had problems with newcomers in the past?" I asked.

"Once or twice," she said.

"What happened?"

Liz shrugged. "There are those who think to take advantage of our generosity, but they quickly learn we aren't as soft as they believe."

While I didn't think she meant it as such toward me, her words carried a hint of warning. Based on the few phoenixes I'd met, I didn't doubt her at all.

When we reached the room that I'd been staying in, my legs finally gave out. I stumbled, and Pavel helped me the rest of the way to the bed.

"Good thing you didn't attempt the stairs," Liz said, grabbing a waiting cup of water and handing it to me. "Time to rest.”

"More drugs?” I asked, only kind of hoping it wasn't.

She smiled. "No more drugs.”

I drank the water in one gulp.

"I'll be back in a few hours.” She pushed Pavel out with a quick wave and closed the door behind them, leaving me to my beauty sleep.

Only as soon as they left, I was out of bed. What I needed most right now was to feel strong and capable, not weak as a newly hatched chick.

I took myself through the paces, flowing through a sequence of training moves and stretches to strengthen my weakened muscles. By the time I finally gave up, I was a sweaty, wobbly mess, and I wasn't sure I would make it back to the bed without throwing up. Years of experience taught me that it took an hour to go through the entire routine, and I could only do half of it today.

Panting heavily, I sat on the edge of the bed and let myself fall sideways onto the pillow.

Murmuring voices stirred me awake. I opened my eyes and found myself lying entirely on the bed and neatly tucked in. That was nice of someone, hopefully just Liz. I hadn't a clue what time of day it was, but I felt fully rested.

I rolled onto my side. Liz and Pietr stood at the door, speaking in hushed voices. They turned toward me as I sat up, running a hand through my bedhead.

Pietr's intense gaze swept over me, and I became

distinctly aware of my body odor and extremely disheveled state. Being asleep for a few days after a battle, then going through a sweat-filled training session will do that to a girl. Thank the gods I wasn't in the same clothes I'd arrived in.

Now that I was more awake and seeing him while he didn't have his hand wrapped around my throat, Pietr was… *hot*. The contrast between his shoulder-length, light blond hair and darker skin was stunning, and that was even before I remembered his rainbow-hued eyes. I had never seen anyone like him before; he was unique in every sense of the word.

He wore light brown leather pants that fit so snugly, I could make out the lines of his muscular thighs, though supple enough to allow him the flexibility of movement. I wouldn't have minded in the least watching him turn around and walk away.

A matching sleeveless tunic covered his top half while also offering a great view of his defined biceps and shoulders. He crossed his arms over his broad chest. This man was in perfect shape.

We all stared at each other awkwardly for a moment before Liz nudged Pietr with her elbow.

He cleared his throat and ran a hand over his beard. "My apologies for my earlier behavior, Veronica. My job is to ensure the safety of Gavan."

"Understood," I said, "but for real, I have no knowledge of anything here. My parents never even told me this realm existed."

He nodded, a move that made the colors of his eyes swirl in a hypnotizing way. "Liz will help you find a new change of clothes, then you will join us for dinner."

Before I could utter a thanks, he was out the door and it shut behind him.

I blinked at Liz. "Is he always like that?"

She chuckled. "Only in the beginning. He still doesn't trust you, but when he does, he'll be a big, old softie. Now, let's get you cleaned up. Strip."

I laughed at the idea that man was anything other than a solid rock, what with his bulging muscles and anger management problems, but I did as I was told. Growing up, I had never really been super modest, much to my mother's dismay, and I hadn't outgrown it.

Besides, I wanted out of this sweat-stained dress as fast as possible. The amount of dirt covering my body was almost like a second outfit, covering any and all blemishes and random freckles. Yuck. At least it covered the weird mark on my chest. Unless it had gone away while I slept. I couldn't tell.

The nightgown ended up in a pile near the door. I wouldn't have been surprised to see the garment attract flies with the stench. If flies lived in caves, anyway. Or in this realm. I had no idea.

Liz moved to the water pump and filled a bucket with fresh water. When it was full, she waved me over to the corner and handed me a sponge that looked like it was made from fungus or moss. Best not to think about what it might be; it would get me clean and therefore was worth it.

"I draw the line at bathing grown adults." The corner of her mouth twitched with amusement. "It's not perfect, but it'll help until we can get you to a real bath. There's a change of clothes on the table. I'll be just outside."

"Thank you," I said, putting all the warmth and sincerity

into the words that I could.

She smiled and slipped out the door.

I wasted no time—I dunked the sponge into the water and began to scrub.

The activity left me feeling a million times better. My hair was still brown, but that was due to the dye and not dirt.

Now that a few layers of filth weren't covering it, the weird red mark above my left boob showed up again. Which was probably a bad sign, but there was nothing I could do about it now. The spot had appeared in the human world, whatever it was; these people probably wouldn't have a clue what it was or how to fix it. I scratched at it absentmindedly. It didn't hurt, which I took to be a good sign.

When Liz let herself back in, I had just pulled on the new clothes—tan leggings and a matching tunic-length shirt, both as clean as the mountain spring air. I wrung out my hair over a bucket and pulled it up into a bun, securing it with the only blade they hadn't taken from me—a tiny knife that fit and disappeared into the sole of my boots.

"Well, don't you look and smell a million times better." Liz placed her hands on her hips and eyeballed my hair curiously. "That's not your natural color, is it?"

Relief settled over me when she didn't ask for the knife back. I snorted. "Hell no. I had to dye it to hide from bounty hunters."

Liz's eyes widened.

"I hid my phoenix nature from the rest of the Community back home until the fae mage I followed here outed me," I explained. "I was the last phoenix in existence as far as anyone knew and a valuable prize for hunters."

Her gaze softened. "What about your family?"

"They're all gone," I said. "My parents returned to the sun almost ten years ago, and my little brother died."

I wasn't ready to discuss Maddox with her or anyone else here just yet. The fever dreams I'd had left me with an overwhelming sense of guilt whenever I thought of him. As soon as I caught up to and dealt with William, I needed to get back to the human world and find Mad's killer.

She nodded. "We can remove the dye tomorrow."

"Really?" I clapped my hands over my mouth before the squeal of excitement slipped out. I thought I would be stuck with this color forever. Or until my natural color grew back out, which was not going to be a pretty process. Let's face it, neither option was appealing.

Liz opened the door. "Yes, but for now, let's go eat."

CHAPTER 5

Tuesday Evening

I followed Liz down the corridor to the last door on the left, which was standing wide open. Murmuring voices drifted out of the room within. Leaning next to the door was Pavel, who grinned when he saw me.

"I was wondering when you'd finally change," he said. "I thought you had a weird attachment to wearing the same clothes until they rotted off you or something."

I wrinkled my nose. "Ew. Nothing of the sort. I just needed to make sure your eyes would water too much from the stench if you planned to attack me."

He laughed, his amusement echoing down the stone corridor. He swept an arm toward the open door. "After you two."

The room we entered was twice the size of the one I'd been staying in, allowing a couple dozen adults to mingle comfortably. Leafy plants hung from the ceiling in pots, and another water pump took up a back corner. A stone dining table big enough to seat eight stood in the center of it all. Platters of meat, cheeses, fruits, and veggies filled the table's middle, and cups filled with water waited at each place.

Two people sat across from each other, a man and a woman. Both had been in the forest when I first stumbled into this realm. Today, the woman with dreadlocks didn't have any tribal makeup on, and I narrowed my eyes as I looked between her and Liz. The only difference in their appearance was the way they styled their hair.

"You two are twins," I blurted, utterly unaware of how obvious my statement was until it was too late.

"Yes, this is my sister Yelena," Liz said as she took the open seat next to the other woman. "No one calls her that, though. Just Lena."

Lena rolled her eyes. "I'm not *just* anything."

"I'm Oleg," the other guy said with a nod in my direction.

His voice was softer and smoother than I'd expected for his size. He was a big dude, all muscles and mass, and his neck must have been the size of my thigh. Scars zig-zagged across his brown forearms and even marked a few places on his face.

Despite his hefty proportions, there was a quiet sweetness about his entire demeanor. Big old softie suited this man so much more than his boss. His hair was a dark red, like a Merlot or a Cabernet. Eyes the color of freshly cut grass twinkled at me from a light brown face decorated with a smattering of darker freckles. The barest hint of creases formed next to his eyes and mouth, indicating a more advanced age than the others.

What was it about big tough guys being softies that just about killed me with cuteness? He was so fucking adorable, I wanted to squeeze him. I gave him a warm smile since a hug might not go over well during a first meeting. "Nice to meet you."

"Likewise," he said.

My gaze kept flicking back to the stone table. There was something odd about it that I couldn't quite put my finger on. As I took another few steps toward it, I realized the whole thing seemed to have grown out of the cave floor itself. I stopped mid-step, just staring.

How the fuck had they done that?

"Good evening, Veronica," Pietr's deep voice rumbled behind me.

I turned to face him. The rainbow making up his eyes darkened as our stares connected for a moment. Besides our first, hand-at-throat introduction, I hadn't been this close to him before. He seemed just as beefy as when I'd been sitting on my bed, and all *man*. Even the scent of him, leather and wood and earth, made him more attractive than he already was.

If only his personality wasn't so cold and uninviting.

Pietr dropped his gaze and approached the head of the table, gesturing to the empty chair directly opposite from where he stood.

Pavel took the seat next to Oleg.

"Is it just the women who get nicknames, or does everyone call you 'Pete'?" I asked as I sat.

The room went dead silent.

Pietr's nostrils flared out. "No."

Liz and Lena collapsed into one another, laughing and snickering. Even Pavel and Oleg shared a grin as they looked at their leader.

"Pete!" Lena slapped a palm on the table. "It suits you, don't you think?"

Pietr shot her a warning glance, but she continued to grin up at him until he grumbled and sat.

"Some of us call Oleg Egg," Liz added, her smile coy as she gazed at him across the table.

"Not Leg?" I asked.

Lena snort-laughed. "Not from his name. It came from Little Egg because he's the smallest in his family. The runt."

I gazed wide-eyed at the big man. "You're the smallest?"

He smiled, displaying two absolutely adorable dimples underneath the smattering of freckles. "Of seven."

Holy shit. If that were the case, then his family must have giant blood in their lineage. I wasn't even sure if I was joking.

"Thank you for joining us," Pietr said, redirecting the conversation. "I hoped we could use this time to get to know each other and our different worlds better."

"Sure, sounds great," I said. "I'm an open book."

Pietr nodded. "First, let's fill our plates and bodies."

We followed his lead and piled our plates high with the feast in front of us. While everything looked vaguely familiar—meat was meat and plants were plants—they were definitely different than anything I had tried before. The smells set my stomach grumbling, earning a chuckle from Liz next to me. It wasn't the first time she'd been privy to the sound.

"As a show of good faith," Pietr said after we had all started to dig in, "let me tell you a little bit about Haven. If it wasn't clear already, we live mostly below ground for various reasons, security and safety being chief among them."

Pavel leaned his elbows on the table to see me around Oleg's girth. "Some of us can use our inner flames to sculpt and shape the rock like it's clay." He grinned at my surprised glance. "I saw the way you eyed the table."

I let out a laugh. "That obvious, huh?"

"Even Papa Boris would've seen," he said.

Lena groaned, a look of pure disgust on her face. "That's a terrible joke you need to stop using."

I raised an eyebrow.

Pavel smirked. "The old man is blind."

I gave him a hard eye roll, but inside I had to agree with him. That was a funny joke—the first time.

"We're a small community," Pietr continued, "but growing. Ivan was with us since the beginning. You mentioned you two just met. Can you tell us more about the incident that led you here?"

I swallowed the bite I'd taken. "It's kind of a long story, but basically, a Winter Court fae named William Caomhánach learned how to perform necromancy. He planned to use an undead army to attack his queen, as well as the Death Enforcement Agency that oversees the supernatural Community of the human world."

Silence filled the room as everyone paused their eating to listen, so I kept going. "I stopped his first attempt, but he announced that I was a phoenix to the entire Community. Before that, it'd been a secret to protect me from hunters after my magic.

"So, I fled into hiding, which didn't last long because the crazy mage decided to try and harness grim reaper and angel magic. Ivan helped us stop the mages from opening a portal to hell, but then the fae in charge, good ol' Bill, captured Ivan in my place."

Pavel let out a low whistle. "Ivan sure walked in at the wrong time."

"Why did he help you fight?" Pietr asked, frowning.

"He said he was looking for something, and I agreed to help him after we stopped William," I explained. "What was he looking for?"

I took another bite that practically melted on my tongue. For a small community, they sure knew how to prepare good food.

"He didn't tell you?" Pietr cocked his head to the side.

"No, we were literally exchanging names while my friends were in battle. I had to get back."

"You agreed to help him find this item without even knowing what it was?" His tone was skeptical.

I shrugged. "Of course. Ivan had proven to be an exceptional fighter. I needed him, and I'm confident I can find whatever he's looking for."

"How's that?" he asked.

"I'm an expert at finding lost items," I said. "It was my job until this mess happened."

"Like a treasure hunter?" Lena asked, picking food out from between her teeth with a knife. She had leaned back and kicked her feet up onto the table's edge, boots and all.

I grimaced. Time to come clean if I had any hope of gaining their trust. "Kind of. I started out… relieving items from human hands."

Pietr's eyes narrowed. "You're a thief."

"Technically, yes," I said. "Well, I *was*. But the items I collected shouldn't have been in human hands to begin with. Really, I was doing the Community a favor."

"While earning a living," Pavel supplied, chuckling.

"Hey, a girl's gotta eat." I took another bite.

"Due to the questionable acquisition methods," Pietr cleared his throat, "consider your bargain with Ivan fulfilled."

I didn't like where his tone was headed. "I gave him my word."

"And as Ivan's superior, I'm relieving you of your obligation." His voice grew quieter, strained.

"But—"

He stood, his chair rocking back and almost tipping over from the forcefulness. "Pavel, please escort Veronica back to her room."

I threw up my hands, a flush creeping up my neck and cheeks. "Whoa. What's happening?"

"Dinner is over," he growled and stalked from the room.

I looked at Liz, my mouth hanging agape. "What did I do this time?"

Dropping her feet back to the floor, Lena jumped in before her twin, "Nothing. He likely thinks he made a mistake allowing you to stay, but he's one to talk."

"Don't tell me he's got a record," I said, glancing at the open door.

She gave me a wicked grin. "Like you wouldn't believe."

Interesting. I was pretty confident they were all considered traitors to the crown, especially Pietr, the man who led them here. I looked forward to learning more, if only to use it as leverage. Some might use the word blackmail.

Pavel stood. "Come on, thief. Time to lock you up."

Although I rolled my eyes, I gave a brief wave to the others and followed him.

"*Ex*-thief," I muttered at the door.

He slung an arm around my shoulders as we walked down the hallway. "He'll come around. We can all tell you're clueless about this world."

"Total understatement," I said. "I just wish I knew why my parents kept it a secret."

"Parents always think they're doing the right thing by keeping us in the dark. I'm sure yours felt the same." He dropped his arm when we reached my room. "Now that you know, make the most of it."

Oh, I planned to.

CHAPTER 6

Wednesday Morning

I woke before anyone came into my room, so I went through some stretches and exercises to warm up my body. Everything was stiff, but I so much less tired. I might actually survive a day without passing out halfway through—maybe.

I wasn't mad at Pietr's flip-flopping attitude toward me; it wasn't the first time I'd been judged poorly for my profession, or ex-profession, as it were. And just like everyone else (almost everyone, anyway), I knew he'd come around.

When Liz came in with the breakfast tray, I just about tore the soup bowl from her hands. I was definitely feeling like my old self again, and that was a fantastic feeling.

Like yesterday, Liz wore a brown tunic and an ankle-length blue skirt that swished when she walked. She was the only phoenix I'd seen so far not wearing pants.

"Not a pants person?" I asked between gulps.

She looked down at herself and laughed. "I hadn't even considered you wouldn't know its significance. Only healers wear skirts in this color. You'd see it more often in a bigger city."

Scrubs, skirts, same difference, apparently.

"How does a bath sound?" she asked while I sucked down the last of the liquid from the wooden bowl. "A *real* bath?"

I almost dropped the dish. Good thing it was empty. "Like heaven."

She took the bowl from me. "Think you can make it down the stairs?"

"For a bath, I'd do just about anything right now." And I meant every word.

"That's the spirit," she said.

I followed her out of the room and down the corridor to the wide-open cavern. We stood there for a moment in comfortable silence, taking in the tiny town of Haven.

Beams of light spilled down from the ceiling holes high above us, though dimmer than I'd expected. It was either a cloudy day, or they covered the entrances to hide them from spying eyes, a smart move if anyone were to ask me. Fewer falcons came in to swoop across to a staircase landing or the cave floor, and activities were much less busy this morning. Only a handful of people were visible cleaning up the kitchen area and refilling the market baskets.

"Is that your only way of telling the weather before going outside?" I asked, pointing toward the ceiling.

Liz smiled. "Yes, but they're also covered during certain parts of the day to keep unwanted eyes from finding our home."

She led the way down the stairs, glancing back every few steps to make sure I didn't fall. My legs were a bit wobbly, but knowing I was about to get clean for real kept me going.

"Where is everybody?"

"We all have jobs to do to keep this place running," she said. "Mine is to ensure everyone's health and wellbeing."

"How did you learn to be a healer?" I asked when we reached the bottom step.

She escorted me across the cavern. "My mother was a healer in Sokol, the capital of Mirfeniksa. Despite our identical physical appearance, it was clear from the day Lena and I were born who would follow in Mother's footsteps and who would learn to fight."

"Lena came out with a sword, I take it."

Liz laughed. "It wouldn't surprise me if she did."

The few people here didn't stop what they were doing, but I still caught a few glances cast my way. I guessed that they got enough visitors or newcomers that a new face provoked only mild curiosity. Or maybe Pietr filled them all in on who I was, and no one cared anymore. Either way worked for me.

"So did Lena learn to fight from your father?" I asked.

Her smile faltered slightly. "No, he wasn't a swordsman. For most of my life, he avoided fighting and conflict. He was a botanist."

Why would that have made her sad? "That must have

been helpful for your mom. Is that how they met?"

"In a way. They were school sweethearts, so when she decided to follow in my grandmother's footsteps and become a healer, he chose to find a complementary profession." She pointed to a new tunnel. "Almost there."

How romantic and selfless. Knowing what little I did about the twin sisters, it made sense that Liz was raised by such caring parents. Lena wasn't unfriendly or unkind by any means (from what I could tell), but she was much more aggressive and straightforward. Their parents must have had their hands full with her.

I followed Liz past the kitchen area and into the tunnel, which angled slightly down and deeper into the earth. The warm steam hit me as soon as we started the descent. My belly fluttered in excitement. "Wait, is this like a hot spring?"

"That's exactly what it is," she said.

The descending hallway took a sharp turn, and a curtain blocked the way. I followed Liz behind the fabric and gasped in delight. The hall opened into a spacious room, where a steaming, circular pool took up most of the middle. The water could hold a dozen people comfortably. Hooks hung on the walls to the right and left, offering us a place to hang our clothes while we bathed, and a few stone benches sculpted from the walls provided a place to sit.

We both stripped to our undershirts and underwear, and I practically threw myself into the water, loving the mild burn on my skin. I let out a sigh as the warmth seeped into my bones.

"One of the perks to being the town healer." Liz grinned as she joined me.

The water was delightfully deep enough to reach my shoulders while standing, and an underwater bench for sitting or climbing out curved around the wall's perimeter. A basket sat on the edge, filled with sponges, combs, and soaps, which we used to scrub ourselves clean. I doubted Liz was anywhere as filthy as I was, but she enjoyed the activity as much as I did.

Liz turned me away when my skin was red from scouring and poured something from another bottle onto my head. She used her fingers to rub it all through my hair, and I prayed it was the dye remover.

"Now dunk," she said.

I did, letting the heat of the water totally encompass me for a few blissful moments before rising for air. After wiping water from my eyes, I turned to Liz to see if it worked. Her eyes widened and her mouth formed a slight "o."

"What's wrong?" I asked apprehensively.

Oh gods, I hoped it worked.

"Nothing," she said. "I just wasn't expecting that color on you."

Dread settled into my belly, and I was too scared to pull my strands around to inspect them. If the dye turned my hair green, I would gut William alive before killing him. "What color?"

"Brown looked good on you, but this lighter blonde definitely suits you."

I let out my breath in a whoosh and grabbed my hair to see it for myself. Finally, I was back to being *me*.

When we finished our baths and redressed in clean clothing, I felt like a brand new woman. The hearty meal the night before and the heat of the water did wonders for my body's recovery. No creaks and groans in this well-oiled machine. Just in time, too, because I needed to make it up a few flights of stairs to get back to my room.

Except Liz led me toward a different staircase, only one flight.

"Am I allowed to ask where we're going?" I asked.

Liz chuckled. "You're always allowed to ask. Doesn't mean I'll tell you."

The stairs ended on a small landing that led into a darkened tunnel. As with all the other corridors, tiny roots stuck through the otherwise smooth, rounded ceiling. A slope to the floor indicated we were going up, but there was no way to tell just how far up we were headed. At least not until the light started to trickle its way through. And not just any light—sunlight.

I grabbed Liz's arm in excitement. "Are we going outside?"

"Only if you don't yank my arm off." She winced, and I pulled my hand off with an apologetic grimace. "And remember, no flying, or you'll get me in trouble."

I crossed my heart, though I secretly thought the rule was beyond ridiculous. Not like Pietr could stop me if I really wanted to stretch my wings.

A moment later, it was like the gods above had blessed us with their presence. Bright light streamed through the cave's opening even though it was mostly covered by some sort of hanging blue and yellow plant. Sounds I hadn't even realized I missed filtered in—birds cawing, insects chirping, and the breeze rustling branches and leaves.

I parted the leafy vines covering the entrance and stepped off a rocky outcrop, onto grass greener than I'd ever seen before, not even in the Otherworld. The sun beat down on my skin, and I turned my face up toward the sky, eyes closed. I drank in the fresh air with deep breaths, thanking Dazhbog above for his divine presence. It wasn't stuffy in the caves, but this was distinctly different than even Miami's salty sea breezes—it was *clean*.

Too soon, but too eager not to, I opened my eyes to inspect everything around me. The last time I'd been above ground, I hardly got a good look at this world before the infection did me in.

While it was easy to tell trees from shrubs, I'd never seen these varieties before. Reddish-brown branches twisted and curved in odd formations as if trying to win awards for defying gravity. Leaves held a bluish tint to the usual green, reminding me of the ocean as they swayed and fluttered in the breezes.

Despite the differences in the way things looked between the human world and this one, there was enough the same that I felt right at home. Even more so because this was where my parents had grown up.

"How far are we from a city?" I asked, turning around to inspect the cave we'd exited.

Boulders as tall as me stacked on top of one another, forming a rocky hill that pushed through the trees' canopies. Plenty of bushes, vines, and moss grew within the crevices, providing perfect camouflage for their home.

"We're far enough from others to be safe," Liz said.

"Do you guys have any cars for just cruising the countryside?"

Letting the wind whip through my ponytail as I drove with my Benz's top down had been a favorite pastime. I hated the idea of needing a new car, especially thanks to William's bounty on my head. Another to do when I got back home: find the hunters responsible for destroying my Benz. I wasn't sure what I'd do with them yet, but I'd figure it out.

"In Mirfeniksa, we have no need for cars," she said, her tone amused. "Most of your technology is foreign here."

"What about phones and the internet?" I asked.

"We have other ways to communicate than phones, and we believe our lives are better, more fulfilled, without computers."

I gaped at her. "Not even for fun?"

"We've seen the damage your so-called modern technology has done to your world and your communities," Liz explained. "Besides, do not confuse a simpler life for a boring one. Trying to catch a unicorn is far more fun and entertaining than anything on your internet."

I shook my head with a smile, not knowing or caring if she was joking about the unicorns. It was a funny image regardless of her intention. The human world had become so dependent on computers, smartphones, and other technological advancements, it was hard to imagine choosing to forego it all. Or maybe they didn't know what they were missing.

Thinking back to old movies I'd watched, I wondered if the people of previous centuries would choose to live without modern-day convenience. Probably not. But then again, humans also had to deal with diseases and a level of poverty that most Community types never experienced.

Plus, they couldn't shift into a bird of prey and fly wherever they desired. Our enhanced phoenix genetics also ensured we didn't get sick often. Maybe that was why these phoenixes lived as they did.

"So, I've figured out Mirfeniksa means something like the land of the phoenix, but what does Mirognya mean?" I asked. "Who else lives here?"

"It means world of fire," she answered. "There are two other… countries, I guess you would say. To the north is *Mirdrakona*, and southwest out to sea is *Mirvody*."

I noted she didn't answer my second question, but I wouldn't press her. If I did, she might clam up completely, and I had plenty more questions waiting to be asked. "Does no one else come out of the caves this way?"

"Generally, we stay underground as much as possible," she explained, "but when we need to leave, we come and go by wings."

"Was using this tunnel to keep Pietr off our tail?"

"Oh, he's definitely aware of our coming and going." She nodded her head at a clump of trees.

When I turned to look, Oleg dropped to the ground from somewhere up in the thick canopy. I raised my eyebrows. I hadn't had any clue he was watching us from above. Sneaky sonofagun, especially for his size.

Although striking in the cave, out here, his deeper red hair and brown skin meant he blended in well with the trees. Blue leather clothing that matched the leaves' patterns rendered him virtually invisible. Only his sparkling green eyes would give him away.

"So, you're saying Pietr still doesn't trust me, huh?" I let the sarcasm drip from my words.

Liz laughed. "Definitely not. That's just Pietr, though, and allowing you out here at all means he's making up for last night. Egg guards this entrance whether or not we use it."

I smiled at him as he approached then looked at Liz again. "Tell me more about this world."

Much to my surprise, it was Oleg's soft voice that answered, "Most of Mirfeniksa is made up of forests like this, except where we've cleared the land for farms and smaller towns. We also have an abundance of water. Some of our largest cities are built right on top of rivers and lakes."

I tried to picture it but what I really wanted was to see it for myself. "Did you all grow up together?"

"Only Pietr and Pavel knew each other before," he said, "but I'm from a small town at the base of the mountains."

A bird flew overhead, catching our attention. It was just a little sparrow, not a phoenix in falcon form.

"How'd you find your way here?" I asked.

"My family raises griffins. During a Haven supply run turned sour, I met Liz, who convinced me to join." The big man's gaze met hers, the warmth there speaking so much louder than words.

A slight pink tinted her cheeks, and she looked away, still smiling.

"Why'd it turn sour?" I asked.

Liz's gaze flicked to the cave entrance. "Our supply runs aren't exactly legal."

Yet I was the bad guy in Pietr's eyes. I guess I had considered myself a bad guy, too, once upon a time, but not like William's level of bad. Just a little morally grey. There had to be a spectrum of greyness, right? I was also doing my best to make up for my illegal deeds.

Something in the air changed, followed by a low hum. A shiver ran up my spine. I got the impression helicopters weren't a thing here, but that was what the sound reminded me of. I turned my gaze toward the sky in the direction of the sound.

Liz and Oleg exchanged a nervous glance before he leaped back toward the trees, disappearing into the foliage. An impressive feat for a man so large.

"Inside, quick," Liz said and pulled my arm to follow.

I didn't know what was going on, but I had no reason not to listen. We ducked through the vines, then turned back to peek through.

The humming got closer, and the leaves and branches on the trees moved in sudden strong breezes. A squadron of angels appeared above the trees. Except they weren't angels—it was a group of phoenixes with wings. I leaned forward, squinting.

Wait, what?

Since when did my kind come with wings in human form? Gold, red, yellow, pink, orange—their feathers blended to create a sunset of hues as their massive wings beat against the wind.

I opened my mouth to ask how they had wings, but Liz clamped her hand over my lips. She shook her head.

Although I mentally rolled my eyes at all the secrecy, I closed my mouth. Her world, her rules. For now. She removed her hand, and I returned my attention to the phoenixes in the sky. A menacing sensation crept across my skin as they neared our cave, the hairs on the back of my neck standing on end.

There were fourteen of them flying in formation, their gaze intent on the ground beneath them. Flying in falcon form would have given them a better view of whatever they sought. My guess was Haven. They all carried glaives— polearms with blades attached to the ends. While I was sure the weapons were just as deadly as they looked, I also had a hunch they were more for formality and appearances rather than used often in battle.

But then again, what did I really know about this place?

Not much, that's what. I needed to catch up quickly if I had any hope of rescuing Ivan and getting home.

The squadron didn't stop. They continued their slow pace over the trees and the cave's entrance and disappeared. Liz let out a slow breath once the droning of their beating wings faded. I let out my own breath, not even realizing I'd been holding it.

"What the fuck was that?" I asked.

"The royal guard, and one reason Pietr doesn't want you flying yet." She grabbed my arm and dragged me back down the tunnel. "Egg will let Pietr know how close they came, but we need to get back inside."

As she pulled me along the darkened corridor, I tripped on an uneven part of the stone floor and nearly lost my footing. "How do they have wings?"

"They've been blessed by the gods to protect the royal family and the capital from attack," she explained. "They receive their wings in a ceremony once they've proven their loyalty to the crown."

"Why are you all so terrified of them?" I asked.

She didn't answer me, and I thought she was going to ignore me. But in a hushed, emotion-filled tone, she said, "The tsarina is not kind to those who disagree with her methods of rule. Their heads can be found on pikes surrounding the capital."

A shudder rocked her shoulders. "Including my parents'."

CHAPTER 7

Wednesday Morning

Did Liz just say what I thought she said? Because it sounded like this so-called tsarina liked to display her enemies' heads around the city, which was downright disgusting. Worse, two of those heads were Liz and Lena's parents.

Before we reached the stair's landing leading us back into the heart of Haven, I reached out and grabbed Liz's hand, forcing her to stop.

I waited until she met my gaze. "I am so sorry you lost your parents like that. My parents chose to leave my brother and me near the end of their lifespan. I can't imagine what it must have been like for you and Lena to lose yours in such a brutal, unforgivable way."

She gave a tight-lipped smile and squeezed my hand. "Thank you. I take solace knowing they died fighting for what they believed in. But for now, it's lunchtime."

My grumbling stomach agreed with her, though my anger still paced like a caged animal, knowing what this woman had taken from these people who had taken me in and nursed me back to health.

I followed Liz to the top of the stairs, where we were greeted with a cacophony of sounds—kids laughing and shrieking, pots and pans banging, and lots of chatter. It was lunchtime for the entire community.

Excitement overrode the anger and fluttered through my body as we descended. This was the first time I'd be mingling with my kind en masse.

We made our way through the small groups gathered here and here. As we passed, more people peered in my direction this time, but for the most part, it seemed more like a genuine curiosity rather than hostility or suspicion.

All the shades of hair and eyes and skin fascinated me. I knew the phoenix kind came in every hue, but seeing so many altogether was an entirely new experience. Like a kaleidoscope swirling all around me. Best of all were the men. They were so *vibrant*, almost glowing or shimmering when gathered in groups. Their brightness almost made the women and children appear dull in comparison, which wasn't exactly surprising considering our avian genetics.

For what seemed like the millionth time since I found myself here, I wondered why my parents kept all of this from Maddox and me. The only conclusion I had come to so far was political. They must have been like these people, disagreeing with the tsarina's rule and not wanting to see their kids' heads on stakes.

Fair enough, but why not just tell us that? It wasn't like we could just waltz back into this realm whenever we fancied. Realm walkers and Community members able to open portals were rare in the human world.

As we passed a small group of younger men, more than one of them caught my eye with an appraising look and smile, and my thoughts turned to Thane. Because I was a glutton for punishment. As much as I would have loved to show him this world and experience all the newness with him—maybe even try to catch a unicorn together—it would never happen. I was sure Adam Larue, the Archangel of Miami, had already given Thane his wings. I swallowed hard against a lump in my throat.

We reached the food line just in time to distract me from those dark thoughts. Liz handed me a bowl, and we took turns scooping out some sort of vegetable soup from the large pots. After the feast of a dinner last night, I was surprised to find lunch so skimping.

Not that I was complaining. They were beyond generous sharing what they had already with a complete stranger, but it was a noticeable difference. I'd assumed the soup I had before was due to my recovery. I followed Liz to a table.

"Do you guys save your feasts for dinner?" I asked after we sat.

Liz gave me a confused look as she blew on her spoon. Wisps of steam swirled in the air.

"There was so much food last night," I explained.

She scrunched up her nose. "Pietr just did that as a show of strength. He didn't want you to think we were weak enough to attack if you ended up being a spy."

Of course he did. Now that I thought about it, their market was full of vegetables and fruits but very little else. They must ration their food supply to last.

"Speaking of Pietr, where can I find him after lunch?"

"Why?" she asked.

"As thankful as I am for all of your generosity, I need to get back home as soon as I can," I said in between sips. "I want to help find Ivan first, but I left my friends and Community in chaos. I need to make sure they're okay."

And say goodbye to Thane.

She hesitated before saying. "Pietr's usually training new recruits during the day. I'll take you to him."

I smiled, relief settling over my shoulders. I would be going home soon, home to Kit and Thane, even if both were on journeys that would eventually take them away from me. Whatever happened down the road, I would get to see them again, and that was all that mattered.

Warmth filled my belly, from hope as much as the soup.

After lunch, I followed Liz through another winding corridor off the main cavern. Thuds and grunts echoed down the hallway.

As we came around a bend, the cave spit us out onto a raised walkway surrounding a sunken, circular pit. Weapons of every kind, shields, and several pieces of armor—

although no guns, I noted—lined the curving wall, held in place on racks or hooks. In the middle of the pit below us were six fighters, paired off for a sparring session. New recruits from the looks of their shaky stances.

One of them wasn't a recruit—it was Lena. Even holding herself back for training, it was clear that she was a seasoned warrior in her every move. She sidestepped the recruit's kicks and punches with ease while tapping places on his body, bringing attention to vulnerabilities.

Another figure walked around the fighters, correcting stances and explaining the proper technique. The man was shirtless, his sweaty, dark brown skin glistening in the light cast from the wall sconces. Blond hair had been pulled back into a tight bun at the back of his head. Firm muscles rippled along the length of his arms and back as he pointed out errors and adjusted the recruits' feet placement.

It took a moment of slack-jawed staring to realize it was Pietr.

Holy fuck.

Drooling would be impossible for anyone right now.

A whistle caught my attention, and I snapped my mouth shut.

"Sun and flames, girl," Lena's voice called out. She ducked under a swing before grinning at me. "Warn me next time, will you?" She grabbed the recruit's arm and flipped him onto his back.

Pietr glanced up at us with narrowed eyes, only to widen them in surprise when he saw me, his mouth parting. Even with the distance, the variety of colors making up his irises was visible.

Liz must have caught my confused look. "She's

referring to your hair. It's quite the drastic change."

Oh, that made sense.

Ignoring the heat rising in my neck and cheeks, I grinned back at Lena before moving my gaze to Pietr. I reassured myself that any heterosexual woman—and maybe a percentage of those who weren't—would have a physical reaction eyeing such an insanely good-looking man. Hot is hot, no matter the gender or sexual preference. Appreciating beauty in any form was natural… right?

I needed to get out of that line of thinking.

He closed his mouth and swallowed, his Adam's apple bobbing. My eyes tracked the movement before following a bead of sweat down his well-defined chest.

"Come on." Liz waved me down the ramp.

Thank goodness for well-timed distractions. I bit my bottom lip and followed her. Time to get my thoughts back on track. I scratched at the red mark on my chest, thankfully covered by my shirt. No need to gross anyone out with weird skin issues.

Pietr met us at the side of the training room.

"Why did you bring her here?" he asked brusquely. I didn't know him well, but I had the distinct feeling he was avoiding looking at me.

I did my best not to stare at his abs, but damn, I was sure he had an eight-pack. The man was ripped. Not only that, but power rippled off him in undulating waves. He'd give Luciana a run for her money for sure.

"Oh, stop," Liz chided. "She's not a threat. Maybe she could even be an ally."

"But first, I need to get home," I said, jumping in before he could argue more. "I left my world in a state of chaos with the Risen and mages. I need to make sure my friends are okay."

"If that's true, why did you leave them in the first place?" That gorgeous rainbow-hued gaze finally fell on me, scrutinizing.

I shrugged, partly to hide the shiver his gaze caused. Literally anyone with a pulse would find this man distractingly attractive. I was sure of it. "I have an issue with impulse control, especially when it comes to my friends."

"Even if I wanted to send you back this second, a portal hasn't been opened to the human realm in years," he said. "Not until the mage you followed did."

I frowned. "Then how did Ivan get through?"

"He's able to move between realms," Liz said.

Ivan was a realm walker? "I didn't know that ability manifested in phoenixes. I actually get the sense I don't know much about our kind."

"It's a rare ability here," she explained. "Ivan is the only one who possesses the skill. That we know of, anyway."

Pietr shot her a stern look. "Do you think it's wise to give away our secrets to an outsider?"

Her gaze dropped to the floor, chastised.

"Hey, you need to stop treating me like the enemy." I glared up at Pietr, stepping closer to make my point. I wanted to jab him in the chest with my finger, but I refrained. Maybe my impulse control was getting better. "I don't know anything about the politics here, and to be honest, I don't give a flying fuck right now. What I do care about is getting home, which means we need to get Ivan back. Pronto."

Pietr regarded me, his face a complete mask hiding his

emotions and thoughts. The man would be good at poker. "And what exactly do you think I've been doing while you've been sleeping the days away?"

"How the fuck should I know? You don't tell me anything." The insinuation that I was weak riled up my anger almost as fast as thinking about William did. I waved a hand at the recruits who were only half-assed training so they could eavesdrop. "Not going after Ivan, that's all I know."

His nostrils flared. "Unlike you, I do not make impulsive decisions."

"I wouldn't know that about you, would I?" I took another step closer, heat radiating off me with my anger. He glared down at me.

Liz stepped in, holding her hands between us like shields. "Okay, let's take a breath. We all want to get Ivan back. Let's make that happen."

Pietr's lips tightened into a thin line before he nodded and took a step back. "Once we locate the mages' position, we'll move in."

"I'm going with you," I said.

He shook his head. "I need fighters, not—"

"I *am* a fighter," I interrupted. "I've trained my entire life."

His skeptical gaze swept over me from head to toe. "Prove it."

I raised an eyebrow. "Excuse me?"

"Prove your worth as a fighter."

"Like, right now?" I glanced around the training floor.

"No, I need to finish training these recruits." He eyed the five trainees and Lena, who was openly grinning at him. "We'll meet here after dinner. It'll give you time to prepare."

As he turned and walked away, I narrowed my eyes at his back. "I'm always prepared."

CHAPTER 8

Wednesday Evening

I t was true that I was always ready for a fight, but that was in the human world. As the hours crept by, I tried to focus on what Liz was telling me during dinner in the common area.

Except I eventually recognized the stupidity of agreeing to fight against opponents I knew nothing about. I might not have been an expert at all the ins and outs of fighting Community members—that would have been Maddox's forte—but I'd fought against enough of them to know my strengths and limitations as well as some of theirs.

But after seeing Ivan fight, I realized how little I knew about my own abilities and how to use them against other phoenixes.

Ah well. I'd gotten my ass kicked before. Maybe it was time again. I just had to stay on my feet long enough to prove I was a worthy addition to the hunt.

"You're not even listening, are you?" Liz asked as we walked down the corridor leading to the sparring pit.

I shot her an apologetic glance. "Sorry, no."

She chuckled. "You'll do fine. Lena told me about your fight with the mages."

"Does Pietr not trust her word?"

"He just wants to see it for himself," she said.

I didn't really blame him. Not only was my skill level unknown, but I was also still recovering from a nasty infection. I honestly had no idea how I'd fare in a fight so soon after, especially because I didn't know anything about who my opponent would be.

Would he pair me against one of the newbies or one of his warriors like Lena or Pavel?

Ugh. The nerves were getting to me.

At least I didn't have to worry about it for long because as soon as we entered the pit, I knew who I was fighting.

Pietr.

Fuck. Of course it would be Mr. Badass himself. He stood in the center of the circle, shirtless once again, which meant I was going to end up touching those muscles at some point. Thane might have taken care of some of my womanly needs, but certainly not all of them. And damn, was this man's body tempting mine.

Not only that, but I was becoming keenly aware of the main difference between Pietr and the grim reaper.

Cheers and jaunts drew my attention, and I tore my gaze away from the very much alive and delightful-to-look-at phoenix. I grinned at the onlookers—Pavel, Oleg, and Lena stood on the outer rim that followed the entire circumference of the pit.

Fabulous. I'd have an audience for my ass whooping.

"Come and show us what you've got," Pietr called. This time it was the tiniest smirk at his lips that recaptured my attention like a hawk drawn to its prey. "Or did living with humans make you too soft?"

Oh, hell no.

I jumped down from the walkway and rolled forward into a tumble. Back on my feet, I launched a kick at his middle. He grabbed my foot, as expected, but I used his hold to my advantage. I leaned my weight into him, then lifted myself up to throw my other foot at his jaw.

The move took him by surprise, and I clipped him on the chin before he could move away. He dropped his hold on me, and I danced away from him with a grin.

His eyes narrowed as he rubbed at his chin, but he smiled. It was a devious look if I ever saw one. He lowered himself into a fighter's stance, feet planted and arms up, ready to strike.

Time to play.

I considered myself lucky that my father hadn't gone easy on me during our mixed martial arts training. He wanted me to know what it felt like to get hit in vulnerable places, and he wanted me to know which hits I could handle, and which meant get the fuck out of there. My mother didn't oppose his training style; she just found it hard to hit us herself, especially Maddox.

We took turns jabbing and feinting, testing each other's weaknesses. Pietr was a block of steel carved into perfection by the gods. Every curve of his body, every hardened ridge, was masterfully sculpted. He was a big man, too, but well proportioned, and he moved with a dancer's grace. A lethal weapon honed with deadly accuracy. No wonder these people followed him, even though he was younger than I'd expect a rebel leader to be.

Ducking under his next swing, I landed a jab in his side. I skipped away and shook out my hand. That move likely hurt me more than him.

"Why aren't you using your magic?" He cocked his head curiously.

"I don't want to actually kill you." What a stupid reply. Of course he knew that, which meant I was missing something in his question. Not knowing what that something was frustrated me to no end.

We circled each other as we caught our breath.

"Don't use it on me. Use it on you." He darted forward, but I spun out of his grasp.

"I don't know what that means." As far as I knew, the only thing my flame could do for me was boost my energy and minor healing. I had no time to wait for an explanation, though, because my opportunity presented itself.

I feinted a jab toward his face, only to swoop down, snag my arms around his knees, and pull his legs out from beneath him. Before he recovered, I was on him, pinning his arms to the ground beneath my knees and leaning my forearm into his throat. "Check."

Our faces were so close our noses almost touched. Warm breath mingled in the air between us, and his chest rose and fell beneath my legs. His gaze met mine, the colors of his irises swirling from blue to purple to green. They were beyond captivating. His gaze dipped to my mouth, where my lips parted with my panting.

I became very aware of his sweat soaking through my pants. I mean, I hoped it was his sweat and not my body's wanton reaction to having a sexy-as-fuck man beneath me for the first time in way too long. His heart thudded against my thigh, sending tingles up my body. I needed to move before I got too turned on to turn off, but first, I needed him to acknowledge my win.

He grabbed my hips, and I grit my teeth to keep in a moan. Before I could blink, I was on my back, the wind whooshing out of me. His entire body caged me to the floor: his ankles clamped down my legs, iron-clad thighs held my hips in a vice-like grip, and one massive hand pinned my arms above my head. His other hand was at my throat, ready to crush my esophagus.

I didn't even bother trying to squirm my way out—I was exhausted and aroused and any movement would just turn me on further. My lady bits pulsed as if to remind me.

His gaze roved over my face and down my heaving chest, every inch of me covered in sweat. A predatorial expression took over his face, and I would've sworn his body rumbled with a growl.

"Alright, big man, let her up," Pavel's cheerful voice cut through the tension, and I heard the others laughing and clapping behind him.

With a last glance at my lips and eyes, Pietr obeyed.

The sudden onslaught of cool air made goosebumps rise across my entire body. I sat up, panting with one arm slung over a knee. I grinned as I took Lena's offered hand. She and Oleg had joined us on the pit floor. Pavel sat on the raised walkway's edge, his feet dangling down.

"You are one tough nut." Lena pulled me to my feet, glancing at her leader slyly. "At full capacity, you might have taken him down."

"Without a doubt," Pavel agreed, a gleam in his eye.

"That's a good point." I put my hands on my hips and faced Pietr. "I'm still recovering. Let's see you try to beat me when I'm back to normal. Rematch?"

He stared at me with an open mouth before tilting his head back and laughing. His eyes lit up when he gazed at me again. "Fully recovered and trained to use your magic properly. Then you've got a deal."

My heart squeezed briefly as his words reminded me of Thane. Making a deal with a reaper and shaking hands to seal it had been an inside joke of ours.

Oleg patted me on the back, stirring me out of my memories. I smiled up at the giant man. It was for the best—I might never see Thane again, or at least not as he once was.

Pietr hauled himself out of the pit and grabbed two towels. He threw one down to me and used the other to dry off his face and neck.

"How close are you guys to finding Ivan?" I asked, doing the same with the cloth.

Lena let out a sound of disgust. "If *someone* would let me torture the mages we captured, we'd already know."

"And then we'd be no better than Galina," Oleg's quiet voice chimed in.

"The mages aren't phoenixes." Her light blue eyes flashed as she spat out the words.

He wasn't deterred by her anger. "But they *are* people."

"People worth saving don't murder other people for fun," she huffed, emphasizing her point. "Besides, I don't want to kill them yet. I just want to make them talk."

"Who's Galina?" I asked. I had a feeling they could argue that topic for hours.

"The current ruler of Mirfeniksa," Oleg said.

"You mean the *false* ruler," Pavel said.

"Enough." Pietr's commanding voice silenced the group, then he gazed down at me from the raised walkway. "Good fight. I'll allow you to join in the rescue once we locate Ivan. On one condition."

I waited, keeping my face impassive though I was dancing a jig inside.

"*If* you learn to harness your magic better," he said.

Learn how to be an even bigger badass? It was an offer I would wholeheartedly accept. I was all in for anything that would make me a better fighter. "Of course. But I also want to talk to the captured mages."

His eyes narrowed. "Why?"

"William was very deliberate opening a portal here of all places," I explained. "It wasn't random. I want to know why. What does he get out of this trip?"

"And you think they'll talk to you?" he asked.

"Honestly, I don't know." I shrugged. "But what harm could it do?"

He continued to stare at me for another moment before nodding. "In the morning. Pavel can take you there before training."

Finally, I was gaining his trust.

Lena threw her hands up into the air. "Why does she get to do it?"

"Good night." Pietr nodded to us and strode from the cavern.

Pavel grinned at me from his perch. "Tomorrow's going to be fun."

The sangria-eyed phoenix was right about that. I planned to make those mages talk, no matter how I had to do it.

Morals be damned.

CHAPTER 9

Thursday Morning

Despite making some progress the day before, I still hadn't gained Pietr's whole trust with coming and going as I pleased. Which meant someone was knocking at my door bright and early the next morning. I had to assume it was morning since I had no concept of time below ground.

Stumbling out of bed, I brushed a mess of tangled hair out of my eyes and opened the wooden door. Pavel and his dimpled grin. Way too soon for that level of perky.

"Gimme a minute," I said to the tall, lanky phoenix before promptly shutting the door.

Liz had taught me how to light the wall sconces using

my magic, so I turned them on now, though dimly to avoid blinding myself. I splashed clean water on my face and changed into the fresh pile of clothes placed on the bedside table the night before. If I hadn't been a virtual prisoner in a cave, I'd almost feel like I was being waited on hand and foot.

After pulling my hair up into a ponytail, I opened the door and waved Pavel on with still-blurry eyes.

"Liz get tired of guiding me around already?" I asked through a yawn as I followed my escort. I teased, but I was sure nursing me back to health over the last week had gotten old fast. Not to mention answering my never-ending stream of questions.

"Of you? Never." He winked. "But her skills are needed elsewhere."

I stifled another yawn. "So, you drew the short stick of babysit—I mean, training me?"

He laughed. "We'll get some *kofe* in you before we start."

"Shut the front door." I smacked him lightly on the arm. "Does kofe mean the same thing here as it does in the human world?"

"You mean nectar of the gods?" he asked. "Delicious life in a cup? The only thing better than sex?"

"You speak my language," I practically purred. "Liz was holding out on me. You must be the real supplier around here."

"You better believe it."

If I didn't know better, I would've thought he grew up in the human world. "I don't understand—if you guys never visit my realm, then why learn one of our languages and references?"

"We don't often visit or have visitors now, but we did for millennia," he explained. "It's a custom that continues to be passed on, I guess in case our realms ever grow close again. As you've noticed, we speak your language as well as you do."

"Why are the two realms distant now?" I asked, following him down the stairs toward the expansive common area.

Pavel glanced up at me. "When the false tsarina's army overtook the palace and the royal family disappeared, she ordered an immediate closure of all portals. They haven't been opened since, but we haven't really needed to."

"What a bummer." I wondered why no one in the Community ever brought it up. Maybe no one even knew about it. I'd have to ask Adam when I returned. "Was the royal family ever found?"

He sighed. "No. It's believed they headed for Mirdrakona, but nothing other than bones has been found."

"Liz mentioned Mirdrakona," I said, reaching his side on the cavern's floor. "What is it?"

"The Dragon Lands," he answered, much too casually for that bomb.

I stopped mid-stride, my mouth hanging open. "Dragon? As in dragon dragons?"

He raised an amused eyebrow at me. "I guess that's another creature you don't have back home?"

"Uh, no." At least, I didn't think so.

"They're as close to werewolves as we get here," he said.

"How so?"

"They can shift into a human form but not completely," he explained. "Our relationship with their kind became strained when the tsarina took control. No big surprise there."

My mind was blown right about now. Griffins, unicorns, and now dragons? And here I thought the Otherworld was cool. The fae kind had nothing on all this.

I couldn't help the smug feeling that snuck up inside. If the Community back home learned about this place, I'd turn into a celebrity overnight, hunted for an entirely different reason.

Who knew, maybe I'd enjoy that kind of spotlight. I could open a travel agency or become a tour guide. I bet I could convince Kit to be my partner in that venture, too.

After a quick stop by the kitchen area for a steaming mug of kofe and an odd, plant-based breakfast bar, we headed for a new tunnel. I kept my thoughts off the bar's mysterious blue ingredients as I gobbled it up as fast as possible. For something so healthy, it didn't taste as bad as I thought it would. Plus, it had the added benefit of quickly appeasing my grumbling stomach.

The tunnel we entered now descended farther into the earth. Even with wall sconces coming to life and lighting the way ahead of us, the darkness thickened. New scents made my nostrils flare—wet dirt mingled with mold and human filth. Thank Mokosh I'd finished the earthy deliciousness of my kofe before that reek hit me.

Unlike most of the other tunnels I'd traversed so far, this one didn't open into a larger room. Instead, a hallway stretched before us and leveled out. On both sides, vertical poles had been carved or molded from the stone, forming numerous cells. Cells without doors.

"Are they sealed in forever?" I asked, not quite opposed to the idea.

Pavel followed my glance and grinned. "No. I can open them when necessary."

"How?" I ran a hand down one of the bars, not sensing any weaknesses or hinges.

"We all have different strengths with our magic," he explained. "Mine happens to be shaping the earth. This cave has been in my family for generations, used as a training ground to hone our ability. So, when Pietr and I left Sokol, I offered it as a refuge."

My eyebrows shot up. "Your family created this whole cave?"

His grin turned smug. "Every last room."

"And you're not worried about your family telling the tsarina?" I asked. His face darkened, and I realized the insult in my question. "I mean against their will. If they're captured and tortured or something. Ugh, I'm digging the hole deeper, aren't I?"

Pavel chuckled. "You sure are. But to answer your question, no, I'm not worried. Most of my family has returned to the sun and those who haven't live far from the capital. Galina wouldn't have any reason to think we went below ground." He pointed to the last cell. "They're in there."

I walked down the short corridor and lit the wall sconce inside the cell with my magic. The light revealed two human figures huddled in a corner, blinking against the sudden brightness. Their once-black robes were covered in dust and dirt and who knows what else.

I squatted down to be at their eye level. "Good morning. Remember me?"

The interrogation was fairly uneventful. I asked questions, they refused to answer. I threatened pain, they called my bluff. So I placed my palms on the stone floor, heating up the ground beneath them. I didn't plan to burn them for real, but I needed them to take me seriously as a threat. Within moments, the two mages scrambled to their feet.

Pavel snickered behind me.

I stood and raised the heat a smidge more. "Who's ready to talk?"

One mage hissed as he raised his sandaled feet one at a time. "How can we know where they're hiding? We've been locked up and left to rot."

"Then tell me why William opened up a portal here of all places," I said. "How did he know it existed?"

Neither answered, so I pushed a little more heat out. Smoke swirled upwards from the soles of their sandals.

"V…" Pavel's voice held an edge of concern, but I knew what I was doing.

Kind of.

"William and his bounty hunters wrecked my car, kidnapped my best friend and me, and caused her to almost kill me when she thought she lost the love of her life," I said.

Raising my fist, I held my pointer finger and thumb in an L-shape like a gun. A tiny flame danced off the tip of my finger, and I pointed it at the mage who had been the most cooperative. "Trust me when I say I have no problem setting you both on fire and watching you burn."

As much as I wanted justice for all the problems

William had caused in my life, I had zero interest in watching someone burn to death. I was confident the mage would talk before my bluff was blown.

Like ninety-seven percent confident.

"One…" I counted.

Sure enough, his gaze flicked between me and Pavel, who was wisely staying out of my way.

"Two…" I pretended to pull back the hammer of my finger gun, letting the flame blaze brighter. I hoped he wouldn't force my hand, but we only needed one to talk.

"Thr—"

"Okay!" the mage yelled, throwing up his hands in surrender.

"That's more like it." I smiled and snuffed out the flame.

Pavel slowly released his breath.

The mage wiped a shaking hand across his face, smearing the dirt. "The fae's got some kind of connection with the queen."

My head jerked back. That was unexpected and should have been impossible. Unless they knew each other before the portals closed. "What kind of a connection? And how?"

"That's all we know," he said, his voice bone tired. "William doesn't share much with anyone."

I raised an eyebrow. "Then how do you know this much?"

"He made a comment when we first arrived, 'Get to the queen. She's expecting us.'"

I had so many more questions, but even I could tell he wasn't lying when he said this was all he knew. "You guys are idiots for following him. I hope you know that."

The silent mage smiled, but neither of them said a word as they sank back to the ground.

I followed Pavel out of the mini prison. The lights clicked off behind us, leaving them in pure and total darkness.

Served them right.

The circular training room was empty when we arrived. Pavel and I jumped down to the dirt floor of the pit.

He faced me and crossed his arms. "First off, tell me what you know about your magic."

Oh joy, a test. "I can use the flame in different ways like a fireball, a lance, a whip, heating things, et cetera. I've also set myself on fire and resurrected."

He nodded. "And?"

"And only phoenix fire can truly kill another phoenix who's gone through the first rebirth ceremony."

He furrowed his brows. "And?"

"And… that's all I know." I felt oddly self-conscious at my apparent lack of knowledge. This was why I hated tests.

"How do you feel after using your magic?" he asked.

"Depends on what I do, but I usually have to give it time to replenish," I said. "My parents encouraged us to train in martial arts and weaponry as our primary methods and to save magic as a last resort."

"Us?" Pavel tilted his head to the side.

"My brother and me."

"Ah. Is he back home?"

I shook my head, allowing the familiar ache to rise. "He was murdered. I found the killer, a hitman, but I still haven't figured out who ordered the hit. We were both supposed to die."

Pavel uncrossed his arms, grimacing. "Oh, shit, I'm sorry."

I shrugged. "Not your fault, not unless you're the one I have to kill."

We shared a sad smile.

"Back to training then." He rubbed his hands together. "Like any other muscle, you need to build up your magical stamina. We need to stretch and use your flame to its limits, over and over, to get it more pliable."

"You make it sound like a person." While I had often thought of my inner flame as a living entity, I'd never considered expanding it.

"Nah. The more you think of it as an extension of yourself, the better you'll do." He rubbed his palms together. "Let's begin."

Over the next few hours, I showed Pavel the extent of my fire magic—again and again. Playing with fire was fun but putting forth so much energy was also mentally and physically exhausting. Just when I thought my flame had extinguished for the last time, he switched tactics and somehow teased a bit more out. I was repeatedly astonished at how long my fire lasted.

Once he knew my limits, we moved into using it on myself while we grappled. The goal was to stop consciously thinking of using my magic and let it happen as naturally as I breathed. That was a lot harder than it sounded.

I flip-flopped between frustration with my parents for not teaching me a skill that would have saved my ass so much easier, and excitement that I was even learning it at all. Had I not been the ridiculously stubborn person that I was, I might not have ever known.

After one of our more successful bouts, Pavel and I grinned at each other, panting as we parted. We slapped a high five. Sweat dripped down my forehead and fell to the sandy ground, but I didn't care how I looked (or smelled). This was one of the best experiences of recent times.

He wiped his forehead with an arm. "You absolutely favor destruction magic."

"As opposed to what you do with the cave?" I asked.

"Right. We all show strengths and weaknesses with our flames," he said. "I'm much better at molding and creating with the fire, rather than destroying, while Liz can use hers to heal others faster than our bodies can."

"I just don't get why my parents didn't teach me this." I shook my head. "It seems so basic."

He grinned. "It *is* basic, but if they were trying to keep your kind hidden from the rest of the world, that was the way to go."

I frowned. "How so?"

"Being overly powerful would've gotten you noticed," he pointed out.

Well, if that wasn't the most obvious explanation, then I didn't know what was. To be fair, I hadn't even known using magic on myself was a possibility until now, but it made perfect sense why my parents avoided teaching me this aspect of our flames.

Pavel glanced at something over my shoulder and straightened.

"She's a quick study," said Pietr's deep voice behind me.

I turned to find Haven's leader glaring down at us from the edge of the pit, arms crossed. I quirked an eyebrow up. "You sound surprised."

"Because I am," he said matter-of-factly.

"Well, you shouldn't be." I put my hands on my hips. "I'm adventurous when it comes to physical activities."

Pavel snickered. I elbowed him in his side.

Pietr tilted his head for me to follow. "Let's see how well you do at more mundane tasks then."

CHAPTER 10

Thursday at Noon

After a quick grimace in Pavel's direction, I pulled myself out of the pit and grabbed a towel. I used the cloth to dry myself as I followed Pietr back to the common area, then toward a staircase I hadn't been up before. He didn't attempt a conversation with me, so I didn't bother trying with him. Instead, I focused on taking in more of my surroundings, trying to understand the people who had taken me in.

Besides the healers, everyone wore the same basic outfit of leggings and tunics, only in natural, earth-toned hues— shades of brown, grey, green, and blue. As far as I could tell in my brief interactions and observations, the different colors didn't signify anything like rank or skill. It seemed more like personal preference mixed with the need to camouflage if they went outside. I should've asked Liz.

The common area was bustling with people, which meant lunchtime must have been close. I thought I'd be famished by now, but that breakfast bar had done wonders to keep my hunger at bay. Maybe the cook infused them with special herbs or magic or something.

The staircase we climbed went up three flights, but Pietr headed into a tunnel off the first landing.

"Where are we going?" I asked, unable to handle the silence any longer.

"You'll see."

As luck would have it, I didn't have to wait long. Pietr opened a door on the left and ushered me inside.

The firelights along the ceiling flickered to life with his magic, displaying shelves that had been built against the other three walls of the room and stacked with books and rolled papers. A few chairs and tables formed from the cave floor sat in the middle of the room.

A library—also known as my worst fucking nightmare.

Okay, that might have been a bit of an exaggeration, but growing up with dyslexia meant I wasn't super pumped to spend any time with books. Even computers were a nuisance if I couldn't adjust text sizes. Reading was all Maddox, and he would be in heaven right now. A new realm plus a library meant I would've never seen him again, only for a far different reason.

"Have a seat." Pietr pointed to an empty chair and walked to one of the shelves. "Along with your magical training, you need to get to know the world you come from better."

I groaned and slumped into a seat. "I'm not a big reader, especially not textbooks."

He didn't turn around as he selected a few titles. "Would you prefer the children's picture books instead?"

I made a face at his back, but in reality, I would have loved the children's books. Pictures of phoenixes while learning history? Yes, please. Anyone who says otherwise is a liar.

He returned to the table and set three leatherbound books down next to me. Each was just as thick as the next.

I opened the first one cautiously and grimaced at the tiny handwritten words crammed onto each page. Did the author never hear of paragraphs and indentations?

"These three are in your human language. Start with this one, and I'll be back with lunch." Pietr tapped the top book and strode from the room.

I let out a heaving sigh and tried to do as I was told.

Three sentences later, I gave up. I really tried getting through them, too. I pushed the book away from me a little too hard right as Pietr walked back in carrying a tray.

He glanced from the book to me. "That boring, huh?"

"Have you read these?" I asked, trying unsuccessfully to hide my disgust. Okay, I lied. I didn't try at all.

He set the tray down on the table's empty side and placed a plate of meat and vegetables in front of me. "I have."

"Alright then, Cliff's Notes." I took a bite, briefly enjoying the savory tenderness of whatever it was. "What do I need to know?"

He sat and gestured to the book. "That's what these are for."

I snorted and took another bite. I pulled the book closer and started over since I hadn't really gotten far to begin with.

A few minutes later, I was still on the same page, my fingers tracing the line I tried to read as the letters danced around the page. Pietr's watchful gaze felt like a brand on my skin.

"Are you having trouble reading the text?" he asked.

There hadn't been a trace of accusation or condescension in his words, but my cheeks burned as I swallowed my food. Very rarely did I get embarrassed about anything, but my struggle with reading was one of them.

"Reading and I don't get along," I said.

He was quiet for only a moment before reaching over and taking the book from me. Leaning back in the chair, he crossed one leg over the other. His gaze scanned the page until he found where I'd left off and began to read out loud.

The embarrassment faded and was replaced with an overwhelming sense of gratitude. Not only did this man *not* make me feel worse for my inability to read the tiny text, but he also didn't even question it. He simply moved into a solution. If it wasn't for his man-of-steel body and overprotective nature, then *this* was why everyone followed him below ground.

I watched his face as he read, the way the lines of his jaw moved with the words, the way his striking eyes scanned the page. He was such a mystery to me—physically strong with a commanding presence yet displaying a strong sense of empathy and need for justice.

This was a man who would change the world for the better, and I kind of wanted to help him do it.

In fact, I was quickly falling in love with this world and the people in it. Yes, I wanted to get home to make sure Kit and Thane were safe, but then what?

I would watch Thane ascend—if he hadn't already— and cheer for Kit when she married Angela. Then I would be all alone again. This world offered me so much more, including a fresh start and a potential future that included children.

I wasn't special here, which might have sounded kind of sad to some people, except it wasn't for me. Back home, I was still rumored to be a murderer and sought after for my blood or magic.

Here, I was simply one among many. Nothing special to see, folks. The anonymity appealed to me... a lot.

Pietr sighed as he rested the book's spine against his knee. "It's pretty clear you're not even listening, Veronica."

I laughed. "Sorry. I'll try harder this time. Please don't stop."

He gave a stern but amused look before picking up the book again. His deep voice swept over and through me, and I did my best to focus as he read about the geography and cultures of Mirognya.

The entire realm was roughly the size of the United States, ranging from snow-capped mountain regions to sunny, tropical beaches. Some millennia ago, the phoenix and dragon kind worked together to build Sokol, the capital of Mirfeniksa. I learned that Mirvody was a large body of water, though not quite an ocean, and housed beings similar to mermaids and selkies, the seal shapeshifters.

Because I continued to interrupt with questions, Pietr threatened to leave me alone with the books if I didn't keep eating.

One of the most captivating parts to learn was about the royal bloodline. For thousands of years, one family had ruled all Mirfeniksa. I was sure there was some bias from the author, but from what Pietr read, it sounded like the realm had prospered under their calm and generous rule.

Until Galina.

The woman who led a coup and most likely murdered the royal family also devastated the world. The cities and towns of this world suffered under her rule, their trade no longer equal as she took more than she gave in return. The dragons withdrew to their mountains and refused any contact, and it was presumed they had gone into one of their centuries-long slumbers.

What I wouldn't give to find out more.

CHAPTER 11

Saturday Morning

The following two days were roughly the same: building my magical endurance with Pavel in the morning, followed by studies with Pietr in the afternoon. Life was peaceful in a way I hadn't experienced since…

Well, possibly forever. Even Tucson wasn't this quiet. The only bad part was knowing William still had Ivan out there somewhere.

Of course, peace never lasted for long in my world, no matter what realm I was in.

Halfway through the morning training session with Pavel, Lena strolled into the sparring pit. She'd pulled her long black dreadlocks up into a heap on top of her head, and her light blue eyes glittered with mischief against her olive-toned skin. She cocked her hip to the side and placed a hand on it, a smirk on her lips. "V, I have a surprise for you. You can come too, Pavel."

I dropped the hold on my magic and panted up at her. "A massage, I hope?"

"Not even close." She snickered at my grumble. "Better."

At this point, I wasn't sure what would be better than a massage—I was physically and mentally drained from all the training and studying—but I never turned down a surprise.

She dropped her hand from her hip and turned back toward the tunnel. "Hurry up, slackers."

Pavel and I exchanged confused glances before we raced to follow her. As we crossed the floor of the common area, I recognized where we were headed.

"Are we going outside?" The excitement in my voice was hard to contain.

"Yes, we are," Lena said, leading us up the staircase. "You need to practice your magic in a real setting."

"Are you sure that's a good idea considering the increase in royal patrols?" Pavel asked.

"It was Pietr's idea," she said flippantly. "You can take it up with him if you disagree."

Climbing the steps behind her, Pavel rolled his eyes.

The tunnel seemed longer than the last time I'd used it, but I took that as a sign of my impatience rather than the tunnel actually growing. At some point, Pietr was going to have to let me fly again. These baby steps of trust were driving me nuts.

When we finally reached the surface through the wall of hanging vines, I collapsed onto the grass in happiness. The ground was warm beneath my body, and I let it seep into every inch of me.

Only a few days had passed, but it felt like forever since I last saw and felt the sunlight. I didn't realize how much I would miss Dazhbog's rays warming my skin, but it felt like coming home.

Lena was right—this was way better than a massage.

"Does it ever rain here, or do I just keep getting lucky?" I asked with my eyes closed.

Her laugh rang out. "We get lots of rain. How else do things grow?"

Good point, only I was too busy soaking up the sun to tell her.

Much too soon, someone nudged my shoulder with a foot.

"Come on," she said. "Time to train. No rest for the wicked."

I snorted but got to my feet. All I had been doing was train without complaint. Okay, maybe a few complaints.

The bushes to the left of the cave's entrance rustled.

All three of us dropped into defensive stances, ready for whoever or whatever attacked. A man stumbled into view; his hands pressed to a bright red wound at his side. His hair was plastered to his dirt and sweat-stained face. Pavel and Lena rushed forward to catch him before he fell.

"Yury, what happened?" Lena asked, helping the man sit against a rock.

"Found the fae... they still have Ivan..." he said between raspy breaths.

"His wound isn't healing, and they might've punctured a lung," Pavel said, his eyebrows pulled together. "We need to get him to the infirmary and Liz."

I knelt in front of the scout. "Where are they? How far?"

"Veronica, he needs help. *Now.*" Lena glared at me. "We don't know what kind of magic or weapons they used against him and whether it's fatal."

"I'll go after them while you guys take him inside." I rose to my feet, ready to follow his blood trail as far as I could and hope it led me to the mages and Ivan. My wilderness tracking skills would finally come in handy.

"Absolutely not," she said. "Grab his other arm and help me get him inside. Pavel, go tell Pietr."

"But—"

"No," she growled at me. "We do this our way."

We had a two-second glare-off before I finally gave in and grabbed Yury's other arm. As we hauled him to his feet, he groaned, his eyelids fluttering. Pavel shifted into his falcon form and swooped through the vines covering the cave's entrance. We were right behind him, though at a much slower pace on legs.

By the time we got to the staircase landing leading down to the common room, Pietr and Oleg arrived to help with Pavel leading the way. Lena and I passed Yury over to Pavel and Oleg, both of us slightly out of breath from the exertion of getting him down this far.

"Once you get him to Liz, find out what you can and meet us in the war room." Pietr's jaw moved as he clenched his teeth together. "It's time."

The war room turned out to be the dining room where I shared my first dinner with Pietr and his crew. A handful of new faces stood along the walls, all of whom looked grim and ready for war.

I tried to take an unobtrusive place near the door, except Pietr shook his head and waved me to an empty chair at the table. He introduced me to the others. "Veronica will provide us with information regarding the mages' methods of defense and magic."

He moved to a map on the wall, one that hadn't been there the first time I was in the room. I leaned forward eagerly, trying to make out the details.

If I was reading the symbols correctly, vast forests covered the majority of Mirfeniksa. Towering mountain ranges sprawled to the north, and a large body of water, likely Mirvody, took up the southwest. Towns popped up across the whole picture.

Pietr tapped the edge of a cluster of woods near a larger city marked Sokol. "They're not far from us, but we'll wait for nightfall to make our attack. As I understand, they do not have the advantage of sensing heat in their vision." He looked to me for confirmation.

I nodded. "Right, but some of the mages will be fae kind and more powerful than the humans with them. Even without the advantage, they'll be difficult to take down."

"Do we know how many are with him?" Lena asked.

"Thirty, give or take a few, according to Yury," Pietr said.

The warrior woman smirked. "We can handle them easily."

As much as I loved her positive attitude, I wasn't so sure she understood what they were up against. "How many fighters do you have?"

Lena glanced at Pietr, who nodded. Still with the trust issues.

"About twice that," she said, "but we won't be able to send them all to get Ivan."

I pursed my lips. "The ones we need to be wary of will be their leader and any other Winter Court fae since their ice magic is so effective against our fire. And unlike the humans, they don't need to spend time chanting to cast their spells. They can use it as quickly as we do."

Pietr ran a hand over his beard, his eyes lost in thought. "Then stealth would be better than a straight assault."

"For what purpose?" Lena argued, leaning forward and clenching a fist on the table in her fervor. Her steely gaze promised death and destruction. "These mages have been nothing but disastrous for the human world. Let's do everyone a favor and take them out before they know what's coming. Before they have a chance to make Mirfeniksa even more of a mess."

Pavel and Oleg murmured an agreement, as did a few others in the room. My opinion was more in line with Pietr's, but I had also faced the mages in combat before. I knew how difficult they were to beat.

"At what cost?" Pietr glanced around the room, looking directly into his warrior's eyes until they dropped theirs. All except Lena, anyway. "Are you so willing to lose your peers—your friends and family—for the chance to attack an enemy we hardly know?"

She sat back and all but sulked. "Veronica can tell us what we need to know."

"I hate to say it," I said, "but I'm with Pietr on this one."

Lena snickered, and Pavel covered his mouth with a hand. The grin behind it was still obvious.

Pietr cleared his throat. "You hate to say it?"

I waved my hand to dismiss his question. "In the sense that I'm always up for a good ass-kicking. But magic works differently in each realm, and I don't know how the mages' will react here. They might be more potent than in the human world."

She snorted. "Doubtful."

"Look at what they did to Yury," I reminded her.

"I don't want to chance any of your lives just to find out." Pietr traced a circle around the mages' camp on the map. "They will likely set up a perimeter guard, changing them out at regular intervals. We surround them and wait for a shift change before we make our move. At that point, I want Lena and Oleg to lead small groups heading in opposite directions to take out any guards."

He tapped the tents set up within the camp, drawn as triangles within a clearing. "After we've dispatched the perimeter guards, Veronica and I will move closer to determine which tent they're holding Ivan within. With any luck, we'll also see one of them using magic to determine their threat level. Should we run into trouble and require extraction, I'll sound the call."

Whether he knew it or not, I was tagging along for more than just verifying their magical use. I might not have known the others' relationships with Ivan, but that kid reminded me so much of Maddox it hurt. I might not have saved Mad, but I could save Ivan. I needed to bring him home.

If anyone wanted him rescued more than me, I'd eat a unicorn.

Pietr gazed at the map for another moment before turning to face us again. "We have our plan. Go rest and eat. We head out at nightfall."

CHAPTER 12

Saturday Night

Nocturnal animals and insects sang into the night as we made our way through the woods. Gnarled branches reached out to grab at my clothes, but we moved too swiftly for them to succeed. The other phoenixes seemed to know this forest as well as the dark tunnels of the caves.

I stayed close to Lena to avoid getting separated, but I could always shift and catch up to them via the skies. Pietr might not have given me the okay to fly again yet, but I was confident he'd forgive me, considering he'd denied my request to get my knives back. His trust only went so far.

We hadn't flown as a group because William's camp was

just a few miles from Haven, and we didn't want any of his scouts catching sight of a group of falcons heading their way. Talk about a dead giveaway. A lone bird wouldn't draw too much attention.

The bastard mages had been so close all along, hiding their camp with magic until Yury stumbled into it. He had swooped down to catch lunch and found himself nearly caught by the mages instead. Only the element of surprise had saved him.

They hadn't reactivated the shield around their camp, a fact which had me questioning what we were about to walk into. Bill would be expecting us now, which should have been even more of a reason for him to hide their camp again.

Call me a sadist, but I kept my thoughts to myself because I was itching for some real action.

Since we had roughly the same number of fighters as the mages and didn't know how their magic would fare in this realm, our goal wasn't a straight-up attack but a stealthy rescue. Sneak in, sneak out, don't get caught. I was basically perfect for the job, a fact I made sure Pietr was well aware of before we left.

We still didn't know what William's connection with Galina was, and I was one hundred percent sure we didn't want to find out. I kept my fingers crossed that the fae would do something stupid that forced our hand to kill him.

A fire's glow up ahead let us know we'd arrived at their camp. Pietr held up a fist, and we stopped, crouching down in the bushes.

My heart pounded against my ribs. I was excited to be *doing* something again and taking down Bill the Necromancer while doing it. Testing out my flame's endurance after all my training would be the icing on top.

From my position, I could just make out the campfire and a few figures sitting on logs around it. Several canvas tents stood within the light's reach, but I was sure there were more I couldn't see.

We waited like that for what felt like forever but was more likely only a half hour or so. My right leg tingled at one point, forcing me to adjust my weight so it wouldn't go numb. As time progressed, I wasn't the only one making adjustments, but the accompanying sounds easily fit in with the music of the night. I held back a sigh. It would have been so much more comfortable to wait and hide in our bird forms.

Voices carried across the forest as figures moved away from the campfire and toward the trees. A few moments later, separate sets of figures emerged from the shadows and helped themselves to the meal prepared at the fire.

At long last, the shift change.

After a quick whisper session, Lena and Oleg disappeared into the darkness with a handful of phoenixes, heading for either side of the camp. Their job was to take down the perimeter guards without alerting the other mages. Once they did, their teams would spread out, ready to sow confusion if the mages spotted any of us.

Between two of the tents, I spied William. His Winter Court features—white hair and dusky skin—set him apart from most others. He opened a tent flap and stepped inside. The brief second it was open, I caught sight of Ivan, secured inside.

I clasped a hand over my mouth to keep from gasping. The phoenix didn't look good—his head drooped between his outstretched and bound arms.

I crept over to Pietr and whispered, "Ivan's in the tent on the left."

His head barely moved as he nodded. "I saw him, too."

"So, what are we waiting for?"

A hoot echoed through the forest.

"That." Pietr glanced around at his crew. He gave a curt nod to the others then waved at me to follow.

We crept through the trees, aiming for the left side of camp. The rest of our team would wait as reinforcements if we needed backup. A dark figure up ahead hooted as we closed in—Lena. She exchanged a series of hand signals with Pietr before we moved closer.

With only a handful of steps between us and the tent, I placed my hand on the nearest tree, waiting for the all-clear from Pietr. A piece of bark crumbled beneath my hand and fell to the forest floor, where it bounced against some rocks and rustled some bushes.

It wasn't loud in the grand scheme of things but loud enough to cause a problem. I winced as the sound drew attention from the mages.

Talk about amateur hour.

"I don't care if you think it's just a rabbit," William's voice cracked out like a whip. "Don't come back without catching whatever it is."

Pietr tilted his head back the way we came, but I frowned and shook my head. I pointed to the tent and whispered, "We're almost there."

His gaze remained on the mage coming toward us, who

grumbled under his breath.

"It's too risky," Pietr said and took a step backward.

But I didn't come all this way, through a motherfucking portal and surviving an undead werewolf bite, just to leave Ivan behind now. I shrugged off Pietr's hand and darted for the tent. I heard the phoenix curse behind me before he followed.

When I reached the shelter, I crouched down low to grab the fabric's edge. I froze as a voice came from inside. Not just any voice—William's.

"You may not be willing to talk to me, phoenix," the fae said, "but I have a strong feeling the tsarina's dungeons will do wonders to loosen up that tongue."

Fury rippled through me, and I clenched my fist on the bottom of the tent, ready to lift it and storm in. Pietr's steady hand rested on mine, likely guessing what I was about to do. He might have had a fantastic poker face, but I sure didn't.

"Oh yes, that got your attention," William said, chuckling. "You see, I've been able to ascertain quite a bit about this world of yours from a few loose-lipped village idiots. I know all about your planned rebellion and how much the tsarina would love to get her hands on someone like you."

A rustle of fabric and a new voice joined William's, too low to make out from this side of the tent.

William let out a dramatic sigh. "Duty calls, dear phoenix."

Footsteps moved away from the tent on the other side, and I looked at Pietr. His lips were pressed tightly together into a thin line, but he met my gaze and nodded. I lifted the side of the tent and snuck inside, moving as silently as possible.

Small candles lit the temporary room. Besides Ivan's form near the center pole, the tent was empty of people. A small cot stood to the side, and a few chests sat nearby. William had been busy playing house.

Where the hell had all this shit come from?

While Pietr moved to the front flap to keep watch, I crept up to Ivan's side. The poor kid's arms had been stretched out and bound with rope to either side of the tent. The skin around his wrists was chafed raw and bruised. Crusty blood stained his clothes and skin, matting down his bright red hair against his head and neck. His purple and blue-mottled face had a distinct puffiness to it, but I didn't see anything actively bleeding.

"Psst," I whispered.

His green gaze met mine, but his smile quickly changed into a wince. His voice was raspy when he whispered back, "Why am I not surprised to see you here?"

"How dare you accuse me of being predictable," I teased as I loosened the ropes that secured him. An anti-shifting cuff enclosed his ankle, and I didn't have any lockpicks with me. We'd have to deal with that problem later.

He caught sight of Pietr and gave a lopsided grin. "I couldn't leave a damsel in distress to fend for herself."

Pietr made a strange sound behind me, somewhere between a scoff, laugh, and a snort.

I held up a hand before untying the knot holding his arm. "Excuse me? Did you just call me a damsel in distress?"

A set of footsteps came close to the tent, and the three

of us stilled, waiting for a fight. The steps continued, and I let out my breath. We needed to get out of here.

I tugged at the knot binding Ivan. One of the ropes holding his arms up dropped along with his arm, and he groaned quietly. Pietr crossed the tent to the other rope, patting Ivan gently on the shoulder as he passed. In another moment, we had Ivan free and directed him to where we had come in the tent.

A commotion started up outside, and I met Pietr's tense gaze. We needed to get the hell out of there.

"We can't shift thanks to the cuff on his leg," I said. "It won't respond to our magic. I'm assuming you can't realm walk with it on either."

Ivan massaged his arm, grimacing. "Correct."

"We'll have to make a run for it," Pietr said.

Except our time was up.

The tent flap ripped open and William strode in. A group of mages trailed him and surrounded us.

We drew our weapons—or raised fists in Ivan's case— and readied for a fight. Our reinforcements would charge in only when Pietr sounded the emergency call.

Unlike his cronies, the necromancer in charge had frigid grey-blue skin and snow-white hair. Along with his icy blue eyes, this guy was undeniably a Winter Court fae. Why he was here, in the land of fire, was anyone's guess. His taunting laughter sent the hairs on the back of my neck standing on end.

Ognebog's flames, I hated that sound.

"Veronica, sweet Veronica," William drawled, shaking his head like I was some misbehaved child of his. "When are you going to learn that it's not nice to take other people's things?"

I glared at him. "Ivan isn't yours to take."

He gestured to the ropes that had held Ivan only a few minutes before. "This suggests otherwise."

"Why are you here?" Pietr asked, his voice calm even though they had us outnumbered until backup arrived.

William's icy gaze flicked to the other phoenix. "This seemed as good a place as any other to rest for the evening."

"Here in Mirfeniksa," Pietr clarified, somehow remaining patient when all I wanted to do was punch the arrogant fae man in his throat.

"All in good time." The corners of William's thin lips curled up. "Take them."

If Pietr wasn't going to give the call to get us out of here, then I would have to do it. As the mages surged forward to attack, I took a deep breath and loosed the falcon screech. I wasn't sure if it would affect the phoenixes' eardrums the way it did Thane and the other reapers, but I chose not to worry about that just yet.

First, deal with the mages.

My jaw stretched almost painfully from the screech's force, surging from my mouth as a blast of sonar-like energy.

All around us, blood spurted from the mages' ears, some even toppling backward, tumbling feet over heads. They writhed on the ground, screaming with hands pressed to their ears as if it would somehow stop the pain. Even William dropped to his knees, a grimace of pain contorting his face as he held his palms against his head.

My magic had definitely increased in intensity since the last time I'd used the screech in the DEA's parking garage.

As the tentpole wobbled and cracked, ready to collapse, I pushed Pietr and Ivan out the back, ducking under the fabric. Creating chaos always helped an escape, so I set the tent on fire, urging the flames to spread rapidly. New shouts of alarm indicated success, from my inferno and other fires sprouting to life around the camp—our backup plan in action at long last.

Panting from the exertion, I took a step back and turned around. Pietr and Ivan were staring at me like I had grown a second head.

"What?" I asked, feeling a bit woozy as black spots dotted my vision.

Shit.

That screech had taken a massive amount of magic and left me drained despite all my training.

"What do you mean *what?*" Pietr whispered through clenched teeth, though I got the distinct sense he wanted to yell. "How did you do that?"

"The falcon screech? Have you not used it before?" I slumped to my knees. "Pretty cool, right?"

My eyes rolled up, and everything went black.

CHAPTER 13

Sunday Morning

I groaned and rolled over. Fuzz filled my head and coated my tongue, making it drier than the desert I had been briefly exiled to not so long ago. I cracked an eye open, my cloudy vision slowly focusing on the cave walls around my bed.

How did I get back here?

I sat up quickly when I remembered Ivan. The world tilted sideways, nearly knocking me down along with it.

"Not so fast," Liz said from the chair beside the bed. She rested her hands on my shoulders and pushed me back.

"What happened?" I asked, fatigue not allowing for much resistance.

"You passed out on us again." She smiled ruefully. "I'd prefer if you didn't make it a habit."

"Ivan?"

"He's safe, thanks to you guys," she said. "He's resting as you should be."

"I've rested enough for a few lifetimes," I said. "I want to see him."

She raised an eyebrow. "I'll make you a deal. If you can walk to his room on your own, then you can see him."

I wasted no time, but as soon as my feet hit the cold floor, I knew I wasn't going anywhere. My head pounded, and a wave of nausea swept over me. I winced and pressed a hand to my temple. "Got anything to help with a headache?"

"Yep, sleep." She pointed at the pillow.

Never before had I missed angelic healing so much. My heart squeezed as Jessa's freckled face flashed through my mind, but I refused to let any other memories infiltrate. Thinking about puking at Thane's feet and him somehow still being into me after that wasn't going to do anyone any good.

I grumbled as she helped me lay back, and I closed my eyes.

"Don't even think about it, Ivan," Liz's tense voice broke through my dreams. "She needs to rest, just like you should be doing."

I peeled my eyelids open at the mention of Ivan. "I'm up!"

Liz muttered under her breath and opened the door wider.

The red-haired phoenix who reminded me so much of my brother hobbled in, holding a crutch under one arm. Maybe it was the eyes. He and Mad shared the exact same shade of emerald. His caramel-colored skin had been scrubbed clean since the rescue, however long ago that was.

Pietr followed him in, towering half a foot above the other phoenix.

"Hey, stranger." Ivan shuffled closer to the bed and lowered himself into the chair.

Grinning, I sat up and propped myself against the cave wall. No headache this time. Liz had been right. "Aren't we quite the pair?"

"Thanks for the rescue." A matching grin covered his face.

Our brief conversations had always been natural as if we'd known each other for years. I shrugged. "No biggie. I had some help."

"Enough," Pietr said and stepped closer.

Ivan's grin fell off his face as he looked sharply at his leader.

"Explain yourself," Pietr demanded. A menacing aura wafted off him like a bomb waiting to explode.

I arched an eyebrow. "This again? I thought I proved to you we're on the same side."

"This is not a joking matter," he snapped. "How did you use that magic? Who are you?"

Always with the demands, this one. "Listen, I don't

know what you want me to say. I thought everyone could use the falcon screech. Looks like I finally have something to teach all of you for a change."

"Who were your parents?" he asked.

I blinked at him. "Really? That's what you care about right now?"

He just waited, the lines along his jaw moving as he clenched his teeth.

This interrogation was getting a bit ridiculous. "Rhiannon and Drystan Neill."

"What were their *whole* names?"

A knock startled us all. Pietr was at the open door with a dagger held ready in the blink of an eye.

Mama Anya, the red-haired woman I had briefly met in the hallway a few days ago, clucked her tongue at him as she pushed past his blade and into the room. She held a picture frame in her hands.

"I thought you looked familiar." The skin around her brown eyes crinkled as she smiled. She held out the picture. "You are more than who you think you are. More than any phoenix. Look."

I took the offered frame and gazed at the faces smiling back at me. The painting was of a family, a royal one judging by the throne-like setting and opulent clothes, so unlike Haven's people.

Except there was no mistaking the woman's strawberry-blonde hair or the man's piercing violet eyes, the same shade as mine. I stared at my mother and father's faces, and mine as a sleeping infant in my mother's arms.

It was *my* family.

The plaque at the bottom described them as the royal

family of Mirfeniksa. Mirilla and Dmitrei, my parents' middle names, or so I thought. It also listed the baby's name as Mirilla, which was my middle name and supposedly an old family name.

"I don't understand." I ran a finger along the lines of my mother's face, refusing to accept the truth of what I was seeing. Tears sprang to my eyes.

"Our rightful rulers were named Dmitrei and Mirilla Vasiliev," Mama Anya explained.

The others in the room shifted, and tangible tension rose almost painfully.

My skin crawled with rising goosebumps. "I see that, but those were my parents' *middle* names. And neither are uncommon in my world."

Not in Russia, anyway, where my parents said phoenix kind first mixed with humans. My parents taught me everything I knew about phoenixes, which had turned out to be very little. Instead, they taught me to hide everything I was.

Don't think about it, don't think about it.

The corners of her mouth curled up slightly. "But they are rare here and only used by the royal family."

I rubbed at my arm to suppress a shiver. "That still doesn't prove anything. I'm not who you think I am. Sorry."

"Whether you want to believe it or not," she said, kneeling before me, "you are Mirilla Vasiliev's daughter and the true heir to Mirfeniksa."

A collective gasp rolled around the room, and Liz, Ivan, and Pietr dropped to a knee, bowing their heads. I sat there like a fool with my mouth hanging open.

"Your Majesty," Pietr said, raising his head to meet my

gaze, "welcome home."

I gaped at him. Then I laughed and continued to do so until my sides hurt. When I was able to breathe again, I wiped a few tears from my eyes. "Oh, that was good. I needed that, thanks."

None of them moved.

"Guys, seriously," I said. "That was funny, but let's move on."

"The magic you performed in the forest, the screech. It's uncommon," Pietr explained. "How did you know how to use it?"

I looked down at the painting again, at my parents' smiling faces. "Like everything else in my sheltered life, my parents taught me."

"It's an ability only the royal family is capable of using," he said, his voice gentle.

That couldn't be true. There was zero percent chance I was royalty, some lost princess, even if the picture tried to tell me otherwise. "I'm sure there's a more logical explanation, like being raised in the human world where our magic must work differently or something."

"My guess is they were protecting you from *her*—the false tsarina." Mama Anya sneered. "Galina infiltrated the palace, manipulating those closest to the crown with rumors of infertility. She claimed your parents' struggle to produce an heir for over two centuries was a sign from the gods that succession through Mirilla's bloodline had ended at last, and a new line was to begin.

"Before word of your successful birth could spread, the traitor launched a coup, and your family fled." She nodded to the painting in my hands. "I took that before I left Sokol.

For months, no one would believe it was more than just a fantasy, and then I gave up."

"But you believed it was more than a fantasy?" I asked.

Mama Anya smiled, tears gathering at the corners of her eyes. "I was the head midwife at your birth. That portrait was done the very next day."

Pins and tumblers clicked into place as I gazed at my parents' faces. All the training to keep us safe, all the secrecy from the Community members, even the bedtime stories—everything was to stop the tsarina who had stolen their lives from finding us.

Except she did. Why else would Jackson have killed Maddox?

Holy shit.

I finally found Mad's true killer. My blood turned to ice, burning with a fiery need to get revenge. To kill anyone who stood in my way. I held the painting to my chest and squeezed my eyes shut. A tear slipped out and down my cheek. I wanted to tear Galina's heart out with my bare hands.

"Would you like some privacy, Your Majesty?" Pietr's calm voice asked.

"Please stop calling me that." I snapped my eyes back open to glare at him. I wasn't mad at *him*, but I hated how I felt—alone, scared, confused. In the blink of an eye, my entire world had changed, and I didn't know who the fuck I was anymore.

And in true Veronica-is-a-hot-mess fashion, I wanted comfort from the one man I couldn't have, that damn grim reaper who set my body on fire.

Pietr gazed back at me, unperturbed by my glare. "It

may not be easy to accept, but you are the rightful ruler of Mirfeniksa."

Letting out a harsh laugh, I set the painting next to me on the bed and rubbed my face. "Not easy is a huge understatement."

"Most people would be excited to find out they were royalty," Liz said with a gentle smile.

"Yeah, well, I'm not most people." I dropped my head into my hands, my elbows on my crossed knees.

Exhaustion still tugged at my bones, and a nagging headache was pounding in my skull again. I felt shitty for my outburst, but I didn't think any of them minded. Through the dull throbs, I heard the others murmur to one another before slipping out of the room.

All but one.

A rough, calloused hand lifted my chin to look into his eyes, rainbow irises dancing in the dim light. "You're not alone in this."

My breath hitched in my throat. It was like Pietr saw right down into my soul. How else would he know how I felt? Unless I was more of an open book than I realized. That was entirely possible with how lost I was right now.

But maybe, just maybe, Thane wasn't the only one I could turn to for comfort. I winced as a brief, but sharp pain scored the mark above my left boob.

Pietr gently pushed me back until my head rested on the pillow, and he pulled the light blanket up to my shoulders. The weariness that had been creeping up took hold, and my eyelids fluttered shut.

"Sleep now, Veronica," he said, his voice growing faint as I drifted to sleep. "And welcome home, *moya koroleva.*"

CHAPTER 14

Monday Morning

I stared at the tiny roots poking through the ceiling's cracks. Crawling into a hole sounded better than facing anyone right now.

Becoming royalty overnight probably sounded terrific to most people, but for me, it meant living in a cage. Being told when and where to be or who I could see about whatever the topic du jour might be was not my cup of coffee. I might've been okay with the whole infamous idea, but not simply because of who my parents were. I wanted to make a name for myself based on my own merits.

The door started to open, and I shut my eyes, pretending to be asleep still.

Liz chuckled, her skirt swishing as she approached. "I know you're awake."

I didn't open my eyes. "How?"

"People breathe differently when they're asleep," she said.

The chair creaked beside me, and I opened my eyes with a sigh. "How ridiculous am I being?"

"Am I royally commanded to answer that?" She smiled at my snort. "Honestly, I don't think you're ridiculous at all. This news would be a big shock for anyone. No one knows how they'd react until the situation is thrust upon them."

I sat up and dropped my feet to the floor. "I don't know the first thing about leading people. That's Pietr's forte."

"It's true he's a natural leader," she said. "That doesn't mean you can't learn to be one."

Casting her a skeptical look, I moved to the water pump and splashed some cold water on my face.

How did someone even learn to become royalty? Kids usually grew up with that stuff held over their heads, every move controlled. That's what I thought happened, anyway. Growing up in Florida, I'd never encountered any actual royalty.

There was an excellent chance I'd embarrass myself and everyone around me in my attempt to learn. Then again, what difference would it make if I was the rightful heir? The throne was occupied. I patted my face and arms dry with a towel and turned to face Liz.

"Ready for breakfast?" she asked, holding the door open.

I followed her out into the hallway, where three guards waited to tail me. I wondered if they'd leave if I asked them to. One of them was Pavel, who simply winked when he caught my eye.

Nope, no chance.

As we neared the staircase, a general murmuring reached my ears. Was the whole town having breakfast right now?

The truth was far worse.

I stepped onto the landing, ready to follow Liz down the steps and over to the kitchen. Except everyone was staring up at us.

As one, the inhabitants of Haven crossed their arms across their chests, fists at their shoulders, then raised their arms above their heads like a 'V.' They chanted something in the phoenix language, and I caught the word *koroleva*.

Oh, hell no.

"What are they saying?" I asked, my cheeks burning as I tried to back down the hall behind me. I bumped into Pavel, who didn't let me escape. The traitor.

"Long live the true queen," Liz said.

"You guys planned this." My tone was rightfully accusatory—their matching grins confirmed my suspicion.

Arguing now would be futile; those waiting had already seen me. I followed the healer down the steps and into the mob, muttering under my breath the whole way. No one tried to touch me, thank Dazhbog, and I did my best to smile and nod at people like I was some real ruler.

What a fraud. I barely knew anything about these people and what they had suffered at the hands of the usurper Galina. I hardly even knew what day-to-day life was like for them.

The only similarity we shared was the fact that Galina

took our loved ones from us. But back in Miami, I lived in luxury these people could only dream about. I had a giant penthouse condo the size of this common area and all to myself.

Hell, I had *two* homes in Florida. Not to mention enough money from my jobs and investments to buy anything I needed or wanted.

I was a thief, for flame's sake. Why the hell were they looking at *me* like I was some godsdamn savior?

This charade was not going to end well. I was sure of it.

Pietr met us near the eating area, and I gave him the harshest glare for the setup. He was definitely the mastermind behind this whole thing. Had I known he'd reveal my identity while I slept, I never would have come out of my room. I would have buried myself under the blankets and died in there.

Before I knew what was happening, Pavel and Pietr lifted me beneath the arms and stood me on the nearest table, earning cheers from the crowd. Not wanting to offend the people that did nothing wrong, I pressed my lips together, hoping it vaguely resembled a smile.

These boys were going to get a severe tongue lashing— maybe even with knives—after this debacle was over. Or maybe off with their heads altogether. I could make that happen now, right?

Pietr climbed onto a chair, although his head was still level with mine. He called out a few words in the phoenix language, called *Yazyk*, raising his arms to quiet the crowd.

When they did, he switched to English. "Friends, Veronica Mirilla Neill, daughter of Mirilla Vasiliev and the true heir to the throne, has returned."

He let their excitement build into another cheer before quieting them again. "Galina Volkov, the deceitful usurper, will be thrown from her false seat of power. Those held in thrall by her dark magic will cower before that of a true royal family member."

Well, that was news to me. She had magic that held people captive? Or was he waxing poetic?

"The rebellion leaders will rise to the challenge of taking back the throne once they learn of Veronica's return," he continued. "Soon, we will return to the capital. Soon, we will return home, my friends."

He stood calmly as those gathered went wild with his words, the shouts and clapping echoing off the high cavern walls in a deafening roar.

I sure hoped he didn't expect me to stick around for all that he promised. He was talking war, and I was on the next portal out of here.

After Haven's fearless leader—Pietr had to be fearless to do what he just did to me—stepped down from the chair, he held out a hand to help me. As if I needed his help. I ignored his hand and jumped down, landing lightly on the pads of my feet.

"Why the fuck did you put me on the spot like that?" I hissed.

"I want to show you something." He took my hand to lead me away.

I yanked my hand out of his. "That is not an answer."

He sighed. "You're right, but I think you'll understand soon. Please?"

The man had the gall to look at me with puppy dog eyes. Only I didn't even think he was aware of doing it. I rolled my eyes, trying to ignore the little flutter that started up in my belly. There was no denying this man's sex appeal, but that didn't mean I would let anything come of it.

"Fine."

He took me by the hand again and led me through the crowd. Keeping my eyes on Pietr's back, I hoped my stare felt like tiny daggers. We reached the staircase that would take us up and out. Now he piqued my interest. Whatever he wanted to show me was outside. I was in, even if it was raining.

As we approached the surface, streams of sunlight peeked through the wall of vines. We stepped onto the grass surrounding the rocky hill hiding the caves below.

Pietr turned and winked at me. "Think you can keep up?"

With that, he shifted into his falcon form and swooped up into the air. The orange and red feathers of his chest and belly provided a bright contrast against the lilac-colored sky. He screeched a challenge down at me.

Oh, hell yes.

One of the best and neatest parts about shapeshifting was that everything I wore and carried in human form stayed put and would reappear once I shifted back. Where it all went, I hadn't a clue. Some static, parallel dimension, but I didn't know if anyone had ever proven that.

I wasted no time shifting and following him. Far too many days had passed since I'd had the chance to spread my wings, and I'd missed it more than I cared to admit. The wind rushing beneath my wings and the sun beating down on my feathers was heaven. I swooped and dove around Pietr in joyful flight.

Surprisingly, he played right alongside me, his feathers brushing against mine every so often. Maybe he felt he could be looser, less worried all the time in his falcon form. Whatever the case, it was heartwarming to see him let go like this.

Another feeling stirred within me, too, knowing that this was an experience I would never share with one grim reaper. As an angel, he might humor me with a flight, but it wouldn't be the same. *He* wouldn't be the same.

Bringing my attention back to reality, snakes of water slid their way through thick forest, spreading out for miles beneath us. Off in the distance, majestic, snow-capped mountain ranges stretched so high into the clouds I couldn't see their tops even from my vantage point. Lakes formed in valleys, and a larger body of water spread across the horizon. The map hadn't shown whether there was more than one ocean in Mirognya, but I'd love to find out.

Much too soon, Pietr let out a short call and started a descent, aiming for a few tendrils of smoke drifting through the trees—a town. Despite the short flight, thrills of excitement coursed through me. I'd gotten a glimpse of how phoenixes lived, but that was in a cave, a very enclosed space.

Here I would get to see how they built homes and worked in an environment closer to what I'd see back in Florida.

We landed just outside the town's edge and shifted back into human form. I smacked Pietr's arm playfully. "This is so cool."

He smiled at me, an expression bordering on a full grin. My insides squirmed in a weirdly pleasant way.

"I'm glad you approve," he said. "This is *Suzdal*. I thought you would enjoy seeing others of our kind."

As I followed him toward the village, my stomach gurgled, though it wasn't the ravenous hunger I'd always experienced after a flight. "Usually I'm super hungry after flying but not now."

He chuckled. "I have a feeling the food we eat here in Mirfeniksa provides substantially more protein than you're used to."

I was sure he was right. Not quite the cookies or pizza I was used to binging.

We followed the dirt road through the trees and into town. At first glance, it was like any other small, non-modern town with one main street. Timber buildings made up shops and homes, their style somewhere between craftsman and bungalow. Cute and quaint.

People of all ages went about their daily activities, wearing clothing like what we wore in Haven. Once in a while, a falcon would flit from one place to another, but it seemed that walking was the preferred mode of transportation here.

The more I looked, the more devastation and fatigue reared its ugly head. It tugged at faces and shoulders, circled their eyes with darkness, and created an overall lack of vibrancy. Scraggly plants dotted otherwise empty garden beds, and a layer of mud and filth covered the bottom of each building.

The few children out and about were the most heartbreaking part. Their swollen bellies protruded from beneath their shirts as they scrounged about in garbage bins between buildings.

"Is this really how people live?" I asked, keeping my voice low.

"This is life for many under Galina's rule," Pietr said. "This is not how we lived for millennia prior."

"I don't understand." I was pretty sure I did, but I didn't want to admit it.

"Galina only cares about Galina. All the wealth and excess that this world creates becomes hers. What she does with it all is unknown, but her people are starving and often living in slums." He gazed at a small child who had curled into a ball to sleep on a front stoop. "And it's worse in Sokol, the capital."

My stomach clenched painfully. "Why don't they fight?"

"With what?" His tone wasn't condescending or rude. It was simply sad.

"Anything." I glanced around but didn't see any buildings resembling an armory. "Why are they just accepting her rule?"

"We fought back in the beginning, but she utilizes a dark magic we've never seen before," he said. "Those in the capital and nearby towns are under her thrall."

"Pietr!" a voice called out. A man whose brown hair was going grey at the edges pointed our way and spoke excitedly to the woman beside him.

As more people caught on to our arrival, we found ourselves surrounded by eager townsfolk, all clamoring for Pietr.

I couldn't understand a word of what anyone said as they all spoke in Yazyk. So far, I'd only learned a few words here and there, still a long way to go before conversations could happen. Plus, learning new languages had always been a challenge for me and my dyslexia.

Pietr held up his hands in surrender and laughed before speaking to each person who had come up to us. He clasped hands with men and women and even gave a few hugs, very unlike the closed-off man that I'd first gotten to know. Liz had been right all along—he was a big, old softie.

I used that time to take an honest look at the people of this town. Their clothes were held together by patched-up holes and tears, and old stains had refused to come out in the wash.

Gazes kept shifting my way, a fact Pietr noticed as well. I just really hope he wouldn't try to out me again. I still needed time to process who I was to these people.

"Friends, this is Veronica…" He winked at me. "A new ally from the human world."

Oh, thank the gods.

Tentative smiles turned my way, and whispers swept through the crowd. Before I knew it, a young woman clasped my hand in hers and swept me away into their lives. They welcomed me into various shops and homes and gave me small trinkets of hospitality—these people who had hardly a thing to their names.

On more than one occasion, I tried to give the gift back, but a fierce tongue lashing or a stern glare quickly quelled that idea.

As the day whiled away, I realized how at home I felt around these people. *My* people. They had no idea who I was, knew nothing about me, and had welcomed me with open arms and a generosity that made my eyes water. They also held Pietr in high regard, giving him space yet sticking close as though he were their respected leader.

For all I knew, he was.

The more we walked and talked, the more he relaxed and opened up. He was kind and thoughtful with his remarks, ended up on a tickle chase with a group of children, and slipped coins to more than a few hands when he thought no one was looking. Not as payment for anything, simply because he had more than he needed.

When I first met Ivan, just before the fight against William and his undead army, I sarcastically joked that his clothing made him look like a Robin Hood cosplayer. I had been so much closer to the truth than I realized, just sans the cosplay.

By the time the sun disappeared behind the horizon, my heart was full and satisfied in a way it hadn't been in years. I couldn't even remember the last time I felt this way. Thane made me feel loved in a very different way, but this? This was family. Accepted without question and not hunted for my magic.

Eventually, they would learn the truth about who I was and sought after for a whole new reason. I'd enjoy the short-lived peace while I could.

With dusk's arrival, we shifted into falcon form and headed back to Haven. As we flew, my thoughts turned murky.

What did I really have back in Miami? My best friend was about to start a life with her soulmate, and while that was awesome on so many levels, it also meant she wasn't going to need me in the same way anymore. She had someone new to lean on.

And Thane? My heart dropped into the pit of despair that was my stomach. There was no life to be had with the reaper, no matter how much I wished for one. By now, he was already an angel and lost any feelings he had for me.

I let the clouds wash over my feathers and attempted to let my feelings go with the wind. At the very least, I needed to return to Miami…

To say goodbye.

CHAPTER 15

Tuesday Evening

The next day went as all the others had—training, training, and oh yeah, more training. Pietr decided to have another dinner in the war room to celebrate Ivan's return now that he was fully recovered. That better be his reason, anyway, and not some excuse to honor *me*.

By the time I arrived after a quick change of clothes, the spirits were already high and likely heavily imbibed.

"Veronica!" Ivan yelled from his chair at the far end of the stone table. He tried to jump to his feet, but got caught up in something, maybe even his own shoes, and ended up falling back into his chair, laughing. "Come sit by me."

Beside him, Liz gave him a stern look. "The least you could do is pretend to have some manners."

I grinned. I'd forbidden this group from treating me any different than before they found out who I was, that I was their tsarina. Liz argued against it but caved by the end. Perhaps I'd be all for it if my parents raised me knowing. I hadn't, so now it just felt weird.

Ivan waved off her comment. "V's one of us. There's nothing to pretend."

I couldn't agree with him more. As requested, I took the seat beside him, passing Lena, who raised her cup in my direction. On the opposite side, Oleg squeezed between Liz and Pavel. Their fearless leader had yet to arrive.

"Pietr told me you went to see *Suzdal* yesterday." Liz smiled across the table. "How are they?"

"*Fu!*" Lena cried with a heaping side of exasperation. Leaning back in her chair, she tossed a foot onto the table's edge. "We don't need to start the night with something so depressing."

Liz eyed her twin's boot with disgust. "Better than finishing it that way."

"It was good to see more of our kind and how we live," I said, jumping in before they could argue further. "I know things have been hard under Galina's rule, but it was heartwarming to see more phoenixes. How long has life been so rough?"

"Things changed for the worse about three years ago," Pietr's deep voice rumbled from the doorway. All heads swiveled to look. "Galina has always been a tough ruler, but her level of greed and disregard for the people's wellbeing grew into something unsustainable. A level of cruelty we hadn't seen before."

As Pietr took the chair at the head of the table, goosebumps ran up my arms. Three years? That couldn't possibly be a coincidence. Not anymore.

I cleared my throat. "A realm walker killed my brother Maddox three years ago. He was supposed to kill me, too."

All chatter ceased, like the air was sucked from the room.

"She must have assumed the threat was gone," Pietr said quietly.

My thoughts took me back to my conversation with Jackson Reed, the man who killed Maddox but failed to kill me. Had he lied to Galina? Had he told her that he took care of us both, which led to her treating her people so poorly?

Correction—*my* people. Not hers. She was a treasonous murderer.

"That mistake will cost her everything," Ivan's cheerful voice chipped in. He raised his cup into the air. "*Na zdorovie* to the true tsarina!"

Everyone laughed and raised their cups. I joined in, surprising everyone into a new round of cheers.

Taking a sip, I enjoyed the way the new drink swirled over my tongue in a mix of cinnamon and fierce burn. Few things made a phoenix feel the heat; this was one of them.

I eyed Ivan over the rim as the warmth trickled down my throat. "Okay, I've been dying to know. Why the hell did your eyes glow in the human realm?"

His grin was lopsided. "I accepted a dare from Pavel and ate some questionable cave moss. I've had weird glowing issues ever since."

I raised my eyebrows. "That sounds like a terrible idea."

The others were doing their best to hide grins and giggles behind their hands, but Lena couldn't last. She burst out laughing and slapped her palm on the table. "Don't listen to the *drochit*. It's his realm walking ability."

"Spoilsport," he teased. "The light activates when I'm parting the particles of the universe to find another realm. Or bounce around the one I'm in."

I raised my cup in another toast. "To not eating cave moss."

The hours flew by as we filled the room with laughter, lots of teasing, and even some juicy gossip as I got to know them better. Tonight was a completely different experience than the last time we'd shared a dinner together. Alcohol was always good for lowering inhibitions and getting the shyest of a group to come out of their shell.

Not that anyone here was timid. The closest was Oleg, but he wasn't shy so much quiet and observant, and even he joined in with a tidbit here and there.

I didn't want to leave any of them, even for a short while, but I couldn't shake the desire—no, the *need* to return to Miami. I had to know what happened to my friends, and I had to say goodbye to Thane before it was too late. We had Ivan back; taking care of William and getting revenge could wait a little longer.

I tapped my spoon against my raised cup, getting everyone's attention. "I want to thank you all for accepting me into your home so easily." I glanced at Pietr with a smirk. "Well, some of you anyway. I can't tell you how welcome I've felt and how much I'm going to miss this place and all of you, even for the short time that I'll be gone."

The chuckles died out, and everyone glanced at Pietr nervously. Unsure of the reason for the response, I did the same.

He set his fork down. "Returning to the human world is not possible right now."

I raised an eyebrow. "Ivan's here. He's a realm walker."

"He is, but we cannot allow Galina's rule to continue." Pietr leaned forward and placed his elbows on the table. "You saw the devastation of Suzdal. It's one of hundreds just like it. We need you to take back the throne before the mages reach the capital. We don't know what alliance they have with Galina."

I set my drink down carefully, trying to hide the tremble in my hand. "Are you trying to hold me hostage?"

"The people of Mirfeniksa, *your* people need you. They need a leader who won't let their people suffer as Galina has." His eyes were understanding but deadly serious. "Your mere presence in this world will encourage others to join our cause."

The contents of my stomach threatened to rise. I swallowed hard against the burn. "I understand people are hurting. They've been mistreated for years and deserve a ruler who can help them. Can't I just name you my replacement and go my merry way? Temporarily, if necessary?"

"It doesn't work quite like that," he said.

"Listen, all I want to do is check to make sure the two people I love most in this world are okay," I said, trying a new angle. "I'll come back right after I check on them, and I can bring reinforcements from the Death Enforcement Agency."

Pietr sighed. "I cannot allow that. The risk is too great."

Cannot allow it, my ass. "What risk?"

"Of you not coming back." His irises shifted to darker hues. "You are a thief, yes?"

Heat rose along my neck to flush my cheeks. Never had I felt such shame from the accusation. No matter how accurate. "*Was*. And that suddenly makes my word not good enough?"

"How does an ex-thief have that kind of authority in the human world?" he asked.

At least he was acknowledging it was in the past now. Too bad it didn't make me any less angry. "I happen to know an archangel, and I'm starting to think he knows exactly who I am."

He gazed at me, his eyes almost pleading with me. "I'd hoped it would not come down to a fight between us, Veronica."

Silence enveloped the room like a suffocating blanket. The others avoided looking at me, suddenly finding their drinks or the walls fascinating.

I wanted to scream or yell or break something. I wanted to punch Pietr in his throat. All I had to do was call myself their tsarina and demand that Ivan take me home. But doing so meant having to take on the role of leader and then abandon my people. Even I wasn't that awful of a person…was I?

I would come back. I would make sure Kit and Thane were okay, and then I would return. But what if they weren't alright? What if something awful had happened and Kit needed me by her side?

As much as I didn't want to admit it, Pietr might be right.

The air turned stifling. Whatever the answer was, I couldn't stay in this room any longer. I stood and left.

CHAPTER 16

Tuesday Evening

Hours passed, and I swear I was going to carve a rut in the floor with all my pacing. I needed to get out of here. There had to be another realm walker somewhere in this world or another mage who could open a portal. I'd force one of William's if I had to. Surely one of them had opened the portal leading here. Fingers crossed they were still alive.

Doing any of that meant I needed to get out of this godsdamn room. The one time I opened the door to check, Pavel's kind face peered back at me. I had slammed the door without a word. Of course they'd stick a guard on me. If not for my supposed royal status, then for being an outsider.

Or the fact that I was a thief.

I ground my teeth together. How the hell was I going to do this?

Sometimes, the light bulb going off in my brain was more like a slap across the face. How had I forgotten the one thing I still had with me from the human realm?

With all the commotion of my royal status and getting Ivan back, it had completely slipped my mind. I pulled out the tiny knife I'd been hiding in my hair and inspected the blade. A light sheen glistened on the steel—there was still some sedative poison just waiting to be used. Perfect.

Now just to trick Pavel.

I wrinkled my nose, not liking this part of my plan one bit but having no other options. I took a deep breath, urging my excited limbs to calm enough not to give me away. I opened the door and peeked out.

Pavel looked up from his perch against the wall.

"I need someone to vent to," I said. "I'm going to go crazy in here."

He grinned. "Vent away."

I glanced down the corridor. Empty, but who knew for how long. "Come in here so I don't make a fool of myself with anyone eavesdropping."

He chuckled but followed me inside. I shut the door behind him.

"Okay, how long do I get to vent to you?" I started pacing again, only for effect this time.

"A few hours until Lena relieves me." He leaned his back against the wall near the door and crossed his arms. "I feel sorry for the floor."

If only he knew the full extent of my pacing.

"Give it to me straight, Pavel. Why won't Pietr let me return to Miami to say goodbye?"

He shrugged. "He's afraid you won't come back."

"There has to be more to it." I huffed dramatically. "Haven't I proven myself yet?"

"It's not technically about you," he said.

I blinked at him.

Sighing, he relaxed his arms. "He's going to kill me for this, but Pietr has this fear that the people he cares about will never come back."

I wasn't sure which part of that I wanted to unpack first. The part about Pietr's fear, or him caring about me. "Why?"

He chuckled. "Why does anyone have a fear? Sometimes it's based on history and experiences. Sometimes it's irrational."

Pietr may be many things, including smoking hot, but he didn't strike me as the irrational type. "Who did he lose?"

He ran a hand through his hair and glanced at the closed door. "His mother."

My chest grew tight, recalling the day I lost my mother. "Tell me."

"There's not much to tell," he said. "She left one day and never returned."

"When? Why did she leave? Where was she going?" As usual, I had so many questions.

He blew out his breath. "When Galina first took control, Pietr's mother went to Mirdrakona for help. She never returned, and much like your family, we could never find her. He's been a worrier ever since."

A rush of emotions swept through me. While I knew how it felt to lose my parents and brother, I still knew what happened to them. Maddox's death was a bit of a mystery for a while after discovering his murder, but now I had my answers. Pietr didn't. He suffered every day, not knowing the fate of the woman he loved most in the world.

As much as I hated what I was about to do, this conversation made checking on the people *I* loved most even more necessary. I would avenge Maddox and my parents, no doubt about it. Galina would pay for her crimes. But first, I needed to make sure Thane and Kit were okay.

Time for a jailbreak.

My face crumpled, and tears formed.

"Oh, hey, don't cry." Pavel's sweet-natured personality took over, and he pushed himself away from the wall. He pulled me in for a hug.

I'd never been so thankful to have a flair for the dramatic... and so ashamed. Having a conscience sucked sometimes.

The last thing I wanted to do to someone who had been nothing but a friend was to hurt him. I hoped he would forgive me after I returned. I wrapped my arms around him and slid the tiny blade's tip into his side, hardly more than a shot or a bee sting.

He stiffened and pulled back, his face shocked. "What did you do?"

A moment later, his legs gave out, and his eyes rolled into the back of his head. I caught him and laid him on the floor. He wouldn't be under for long, just long enough to make my escape.

Grabbing the cloak Liz had gifted me, I threw it around my shoulders and pulled the hood over my head. I opened the door, peering out cautiously. The hallway was empty. I took a deep breath and willed myself to go—it was now or never.

Moving as quickly as I dared to avoid making any sounds, I hurried down the hall and staircase leading into the common area. Dinnertime had come and gone long ago, which meant the cavern was all but deserted.

I crossed the floor to the stairs that would lead me up and out, trying not to rush and draw attention from the few people cleaning up. Through my conversations with Pavel while training, I knew the ceiling holes used for falcon form were covered at night for further protection. There was only one way in and out for would-be attackers.

Sure I was about to get caught at any moment, my heartbeat pounded in my eardrums. It couldn't be this easy. Pietr considered me a lowly thief after all.

Halfway up the last part of the ramp, just when I started to get overly confident, I ran into my second real obstacle. Two sets of footsteps echoed down the tunnel, coming my way in the dark. I pressed myself against the wall, urging my racing heart to slow.

"We can't keep her locked up forever," Ivan's voice reached my ears.

Well, fuck. My luck had run out.

Hoping the shadows would hide my presence, I shifted into bird form and swooped up to a small crevice in the stone, barely large enough for me to squeeze in and cling with my talons.

Pietr sighed just as the two men stepped into view. "I know."

Judging by their dark clothing, they must be coming in from their watch.

"We'll find another way," Ivan said. "My family is strong. They'll survive her worst. I know it." Despite the strong sentiment, his voice cracked with the last word.

"Why not tell her what Galina has done to your mother?" Pietr asked gently. "And your sister?"

My tiny body trembled, and I gripped the stone tighter. What did he mean?

Ivan shook his head. "I'm not going to guilt her anymore. If she doesn't care enough about her people to stay, why would my family's imprisonment be any different?"

The two men moved out of sight just in time. I dropped like a stone to the floor, shifting back to human form and falling to my knees. My breaths came out hard and fast as if the air was stolen from me.

He was right. Checking on two people who had all the help they could get was beyond selfish. I couldn't leave these people in such dire straits, even for a short time. Not just these people, but *my* people. Getting me to see that shouldn't have taken learning about Ivan's family. I should care about every single person in Mirfeniksa, as their tsarina.

Or, you know, as a decent person.

Shame flushed its way across my face and settled across my shoulders, weighing me down.

I wasn't a leader. I didn't know the first thing about leading anyone. Hell, I couldn't even keep Mad alive. After figuring out Galina's involvement, I knew that wasn't entirely due to my lack of adulting and leadership abilities, but knowing that didn't make me feel any better. I guess I would have to learn to lead.

Ugh. Lessons like this could be so hard to swallow.

By the time I snuck back to my room and hung up my cloak, Pavel started to stir. I helped him sit up, and he looked at me with confusion.

"Why am I in here?" he asked. "And sleeping?"

One of the best perks of my poison was a minor loss of short-term memory.

"You came in to listen to me vent, then you fainted," I said. "Was I that boring, or did you not get enough to eat today?"

"I guess not." Grumbling, he ran a hand through his golden hair. He looked at me sheepishly. "Do me a favor and don't tell the others, yeah?"

I smiled. "I wouldn't dream of it."

CHAPTER 17

Wednesday Morning

I sucked up my courage, tucked away my pride, and met with Pietr first thing in the morning. Okay, technically, he met with me in my room after I summoned him.

Today, he was back in his light tan leggings and tunic, a color that showed off the lines of his muscular legs and the dark brown skin of his biceps. He stood across from me with his arms crossed, his expression a perfect mask hiding whatever feelings he had deep inside. The only part of him shifting was the color of his eyes.

"Listen," I said and took a deep breath, "I know my behavior last night was less than ideal, but I've come to terms with my role here. I'll help."

Pietr uncrossed his arms, and his gaze softened. "Thank you. The people of Mirfeniksa deserve better, far better than Galina. Being a leader may be a new and foreign idea for you, but we believe in you. *I* believe in you."

"You believe in a thief?" I asked, smiling.

The corner of his mouth twitched. "You've proven to be far more than that. Besides, you're an ex-thief, right?"

"You do realize that you'll actually be the one leading, right?" I asked, ignoring the tingles spreading in my belly. There was only one man my heart wanted, my body's reaction be damned. "I'll just be the face of it all."

"A far more beautiful face than mine," he said.

"Flattery only gets you so far." Even if my heart performed a little pitter-patter. Working with him was going to be tough.

He chuckled. "Well, I'm glad you're staying because I have a feeling that you're going to like what comes next."

"Which is what?" I asked eagerly. I was such a sucker for surprises.

"Come with me." He nodded his head toward the door. "I'm willing to bet your parents never taught you how to speak long distance with other phoenixes, without human technology."

As we walked, my pulse raced faster with the suggestion behind his words. "That would be a correct assumption."

"No big surprise, but we can use fire to communicate." He opened his hand toward the war room.

I stepped inside. Everyone else was already gathered and looked up at me with a mixture of relief and humor.

Reaching across the table, Lena held out a hand to Pavel. "Pay up."

He grumbled and produced some coins, which he placed in her palm.

I glared up at Pietr. "You knew I would change my mind?"

He smiled. "I had hope. But now that we're all here, let's get down to business."

Narrowing my eyes at Pavel for betting against me, I took my now standard seat between Lena and Ivan, who sat at the table's far end. Liz and Pavel sat across from me, and Oleg stood by the door.

Pietr remained standing, placing his hands on the back of his chair at the head of the table. He looked around the room, meeting each of our gazes in turn.

"This is it," he said at last. "The moment we've been waiting for. The rightful tsarina has returned, ready to take her place and depose the tyrant who has tried to bring us to our knees." His knuckles whitened as he gripped the back of the chair. "Even on our knees, we have not given up. We will show her what the true strength of will and character is. We will show her that no matter how hard she tries to beat us down, the phoenix rises again."

The others pounded their fists on the table with shouts of encouragement.

Pietr looked at Ivan. "Let Katya know she can notify the others."

With a whoop, he jumped to his feet and trotted out of the room.

I wracked my brain but couldn't put a face or job to the name. "Who's Katya?"

"Our birdkeeper," Lena said. "Speaking with other birds is her specialty, and all the rebellion leaders keep one on staff. Way safer than paper."

I loved how casually they explained these things, as if speaking with birds were a normal part of life. It was one thing to understand each other's falcon screeches, but our communication skills didn't reach beyond that. Except they did for some, apparently.

"The messages will let the others know we are ready to act," Pietr continued. "Once we receive confirmation from each of them, we will convene through the ritual fire."

"How long will confirmation take?" I asked.

"A few hours at most," Lena said. "Our birds are swift, and none of us are far from the capital."

I frowned, not wanting to wait any longer to experience a new use of magic. Not to mention seeing this whole plan through. "Why not reach out with the ritual fire magic you just told me about?"

"As with all magic, it has its limitations," Oleg's quiet voice explained from his place by the door. "Both parties must be ready and waiting with fire to communicate."

"Do you think Adrik will join us?" Lena asked, her lip curling up. "He's been very vocal about his hesitations."

Pietr sighed. "He will join the call to meet if only to voice his dissent once again. Whether or not he will join the fight?" He let the question hang in the air.

"Why wouldn't he?" I asked, vaguely recalling the man's name from my studies, along with the three other rebellion leaders.

All four oversaw the quadrants making up Mirfeniksa's land, with Pietr handling the middle, forested area. If I remembered correctly, Adrik's region bordered the dragon lands to the northeast and included Sokol.

"His land is among the most prosperous, especially under Galina's rule," Pavel explained. "He'll never risk harming it."

"We have to put our faith in him to do the right thing," Liz said, her heartfelt tone making me smile. "Especially once he learns of Veronica's return."

"You honestly believe he'll do the right thing?" Pavel laughed. "Sorry, Liz, but you've lost your mind."

"Or maybe I'm just a firm believer in good," she said.

"If only more feniksy were like you." He reached over the empty seat between them and tapped her on the nose.

I glanced at Oleg just in time to see the gentle giant of a man stand straighter by the door, a hint of a smile curving his lips. The dude was crushing hard.

"Our only option at this point is to continue as if he will join us," Pietr said. "Let's get back to work until we receive responses."

Everyone rose to leave the room, and I stood with them.

Pietr held up a hand to stop me. "May I have a word with you first?"

I sat again, a little wary of what he was going to say. "Sure."

Once we were alone, he leaned his forearms on his chair's back and met my gaze. "It's been brought to my attention that you have a surviving family member in Mirfeniksa."

I blinked at him as my body did all kinds of weird things internally. My pulse raced, my head went kind of fuzzy, and I felt like I might throw up. It wouldn't be the first time I threw up on an attractive man's feet.

I swallowed hard and asked, "Who?"

"An aunt on your mother's side," he said.

Holy shit.

I couldn't believe I had family, an actual blood relative. And not just any relative, but my mom's sister. My breath hitched in my throat. All the stories she'd be able to tell me about their lives growing up.

"How long have you known?" I asked.

"Only since Wednesday evening."

I snapped my eyes up to look at him. "Why didn't you tell me earlier?"

"The last thing I wanted to do was make you feel even more trapped," he explained, firmly but gently. "I would have told you before you left, but I had a feeling you'd change your mind about staying. I didn't want to add any pressure before you made that decision."

My stomach did a little flip-flop, and my body warmed beneath his gaze. This man was seriously blowing my expectations out of the water, and the more time I spent with him, the more I didn't want to leave this world—ever. And now knowing I had family here?

I refused to let other memories surface, try as they might. Like the scent of lingering cardamon after stolen moments. The taste of salt and ocean breezes during passionate kisses.

Nothing could come of those memories except heartache.

"I'd like to meet her before we take back the capital," I said, rubbing at the familiar tingling spot on my chest.

Pietr smiled. "I've already asked that she be present after the conversation with the other leaders tonight. We'll need to keep her identity concealed for safety until after we announce your presence to the rest of the world."

I nodded. "What's her name?"

"Zasha."

My heart swelled with excitement and pride. I had an aunt.

CHAPTER 18

Wednesday Evening

By the time evening arrived, we'd received all but one response—no big surprise on who hadn't bothered to reply. Adrik was going to be a problem. How big of a problem was yet to be determined. Hopefully, we'd get some clarity during the meeting.

I was about to open my door and head to the war room when Liz popped in.

She held a wrapped bundle in her arms and smiled at me. "I have a gift for you." She laid the package on the bed and carefully opened it.

The confusion pulling my eyebrows together melted into astonishment. Inside sat a complete set of brand-new leather armor. A rich, earthy scent curled around me as it drifted off the pieces.

"I had them specially tailored for you," she said. "Will you wear them tonight?"

"I would be honored." I blinked away the moisture collecting in my eyes. "But you'll have to help me figure it all out. I've never worn actual armor before."

As she helped me into them, each piece fit perfectly as if the tanner had measured me to the exact millimeter. Come to think of it, Liz could have easily measured me while I slept off the werewolf infection, though why she would have before she knew my identity was anyone's guess. Her meticulous nature wasn't exactly a secret. She'd had to get me new clothes, after all.

The leather was dyed black, a sultry color that suited me quite well and set me apart from all the others in their tans, blues, and greens. I got the distinct sense Liz knew me far better than I gave her credit for. The tanner had also carved and dyed a roaring flame design into the reinforced bits of armor, like the pauldrons and greaves.

After the last piece was in place, only a smaller wrapped item that Liz had hidden beneath everything else remained. She picked it up and unwrapped it—a delicate tiara. The maker had twisted the metal to form swirling flames, coming together in the middle and rising into a phoenix, wings spread.

She met my wide-eyed gaze with a knowing smile. "I knew you wouldn't go for anything fancier, more fitting for a tsarina."

I smiled back. She was absolutely right. "You're lucky I like you enough to wear this one."

She motioned for me to sit on the chair. When I did, she took the small crown in her hands and placed it on my head. Thankfully, I barely felt the weight of the thing. She deftly braided my hair, securing the ends of the tiara in loops of my hair. She stood back and admired her handiwork with an approving smile. "Ready?"

"Not really," I said.

She rolled her eyes. "That's the spirit."

Grinning, I followed her out of the room.

Pavel pushed himself off the wall beside the door, his maroon-colored eyes widening. He dipped his head. "Your Majesty."

"Ugh." I held up a hand. "I'm going to take all this off right now if you start doing *that*."

He smirked. "I won't argue with you taking everything off."

Liz gasped and might have clutched at her pearls had she been wearing any, but I just laughed and motioned for him to lead the way.

When we reached the stairs, two phoenixes I knew as warriors fell in behind our group. I followed Pavel through the main cavern with Liz at my side, doing my best to ignore the whispers and quick bows as I passed. For the most part, everyone respected my request to treat me like they had before the revelation, but I didn't fault anyone who couldn't help themselves.

I was also very thankful the dinner crowd had already come and gone.

Down a narrow and winding hallway off the common area, we arrived in a new cavern. This one was open and expansive, the ceiling a few dozen feet above us but empty of anything besides a roaring fire built in a massive fireplace on one wall. A group of phoenixes huddled together near the light, talking quietly.

Lena wore half her black dreadlocks up in a giant bun. Despite the extra height of her hair, she stood dwarfed next to Oleg, who clasped his hands behind his back. Puffy pink scars laced across the dark skin of his arms. Ivan and Pietr had both worn their shoulder-length hair down, but where Pietr's was as white-blond as mine, Ivan's was as red as the fire behind him.

Not just a group of phoenixes.

My friends.

Blue, green, and rainbow-hued gazes focused on me approaching, and the chatter quickly ceased. They bowed as one.

I raised my hands and motioned for them to stand straight. "Oh, stop. I'm still the same Veronica. I'm still just me."

Pietr's gaze swept over me, something like pride shining in his eyes. "You'll never be *just* anything."

My heart thumped wildly, and I found myself lost for words for the first time in… ever?

"You're going to have to get used to it eventually." Ivan leaned his arm on Lena's shoulder.

Thank goodness for the kid snapping me out of it.

"No need to rush it," I said. "Has Adrik responded?"

Pietr shook his head. "I didn't expect him to, but he'll most likely attend the meeting anyway."

"Do they know about me?"

His grin was almost wicked, a most delightful look for him. "No. You'll be the big surprise."

I nodded. "Let's do it then."

Pietr glanced at Oleg, who stood directly beside the fireplace. The bigger man closed his eyes, his hands still clasped behind him. If I didn't know better, I'd say he was meditating. Actually, I didn't know better.

Lena must have caught my confused expression because she leaned close to whisper, "The silent types are the best at fire communication. Don't ask me why."

"How does this work exactly?" I asked, genuinely curious.

"See that symbol?" She pointed to the floor.

My gaze followed her finger, seeing only stone until the faintest hint of color sparkled in the moving flames' light. An entire design slowly appeared as I let my eyes adjust, the whole thing roughly ten feet across and looping through the fireplace. A circle took up the design's middle. Because the image was so faint, I didn't even notice it when I first walked in.

"What does it mean?" I asked.

Lena shrugged. "Nothing, in particular. Just a symbol from the old days, I think. But Pietr shares the symbol with the others, and their flame speakers use it to tie our fires together."

How fascinating. "And then we can all see each other?"

"Others can only see you if you stand within the central circle, but those remaining outside of it can still see and hear everything going on inside," she said. "This is why you want to trust the people using it."

I watched Oleg's freckled face for any hint of what he was doing, but every muscle of the big man's body was as still as a statue.

The symbol painted on the floor began to glow. As he continued to concentrate, fire sped out of the fireplace, snaking its way around the marks like a domino effect. The blaze grew in intensity and large enough to encompass a dozen or so people within the center. Flames built higher and brighter, warming the room.

Pietr faced me. "I'll talk to them first. When I turn to you again, that will be your cue to step inside."

I nodded, swallowing against the nerves growing inside my body.

Taking my hands in his, he brought them to his lips. He kissed my knuckles and smiled, sending a dizzying number of butterflies into a spritely jig in my stomach. "Just be you. You are the true tsarina, and you will be spectacular."

After he released my hands and turned away, Lena elbowed me in the side. I gave her an innocent look, and she winked at me.

Oh, flames. I was in trouble.

Pietr stepped through the circle of fire and stood tall, his arms crossed across his broad chest.

Patience wasn't one of the virtues I possessed much of, so I was thankful we didn't have to wait long. Three figures coalesced into view as if out of the flames themselves. Each greeted him with a nod or a smile. Except, unlike Pietr, their bodies remained see-through and filled with swirling smoke, making it clear who was physically present in our cavern.

The three newcomers were women, a fact I'd learned during one of my library sessions with Pietr. Mirfeniksa was a matriarchal society.

Feodora, Mila, Taisiya. I'd forced myself to memorize the rebel leaders' names. Each was easily identifiable based on what he'd told me.

I walked around the circle, appraising each attendee with a general sense of awe at this mode of communication. Even though I was raised with magic and dealt with it in the Community population back home, seeing something new in action always fascinated me.

Feodora was tall and lithe, built with a ballerina's body and grace. She held her head high, dark brown hair streaked with white tied up in a high ponytail. Along with pale, cream-colored skin, her contrasting attributes accentuated her deep blue eyes and the minor crow's feet forming beside them. According to Pietr, she was nearing her return to the sun but didn't want to leave before unseating Galina.

Mila was just as tall, only twice as wide and made of solid brick. She wove her silvery-white hair into a multitude of braids against her scalp before flowing loosely in waves around her shoulders. Thick white eyebrows arched dramatically above golden eyes, which surveyed the area as intensely as she would in falcon form. Her skin was as tough as the rest of her, a beautifully tanned leather scored from battle.

In looks, Taisiya was as much their opposite as light was to dark and the youngest. She was pint-sized, smaller even than Angela. Fiery red curls blazed out around her head like the sun. Her skin was more naturally brown than tan and covered in splatters of darker freckles like Oleg's. The feature that almost made my jaw drop was her eyes—they were as blazing red as her hair. If anyone could claim to be god-touched, it would be her.

Despite their differences in age and appearances, each woman exuded confidence in her position, rocking scars and armor like they had been born into their roles. I admired them even more for it.

In my limited studies, we'd reviewed the work they did for the rebellion, including intercepting supply shipments headed for the capital and redistributing the goods to those most in need. I wanted to get to know them better, ask them for advice in becoming a leader, or just shoot the shit for a while. Maybe I would have that chance after we won the fight.

Feodora asked a question in Yazyk, her words sharp and concise. She spoke so fast, I only caught one word: Adrik, the missing leader.

"Whether he joins us or not is no longer a concern of mine," Pietr said. "I'll address you all in one of the human languages today, the reason for which will become clear shortly."

The three women shared looks of curiosity, but none spoke against his wish.

"The time has arrived for us to move against Galina and the capital," he continued, the others' eyes widening.

"I did not think we had the forces," Mila said, her voice deep and gravelly. Befitting for a woman her size. She rested her hands on her generous hips.

"We will once word spreads," he said.

A fourth smoky figure stepped into the circle, this time a man. This must be Adrik.

Like Feodora and Mila, he showed hints of aging, which meant he was likely a few hundred years old—middle-aged for our kind. He had pulled his long auburn hair up into a tight bun on the crown of his head, a few streaks of silver flashing through the gold and red. As for the rest of him, he was built like a tank. Thick arms, each the size of one of my thighs, crossed over a rock-solid chest. I'd be willing to bet his thighs were as wide as my torso, and I couldn't tell who was taller, him or Pietr.

Shrewd purple eyes regarded the others with an air of hostility and condescension I instantly disliked. His gaze spoke volumes, as if he were somehow more important than anyone else. I hated that he shared a similar eye color to mine.

I clenched my fists, itching to put him in his place with a solid strike to the balls. Plenty of time for that later, *if* he survived the battle, which I kind of hoped he didn't right about now.

I never claimed to be a saint.

"Adrik, it's good of you to join us," Pietr said.

The behemoth of a man glared at Pietr across the circle. His booming voice lashed out in Yazyk, demanding and cold, whatever it was he said.

Beside me, Lena uncrossed her arms and muttered under her breath.

"What'd he say?" I whispered.

"That Pietr is demeaning him by speaking in a human language." She glanced at me. "This may not go as well as he hopes."

Right.

Pursing my lips, I decided not to wait any longer. I took a deep breath, exhaled, then stepped through the flames and into the circle beside Pietr. Meeting Adrik's gaze full-on, I waited for him to take in my appearance. Recognition flared to life in his eyes.

"What is the meaning of this?" Taisiya asked, her red

eyes opened wide.

Pietr took a step back and bowed in my direction. "Comrades, this is Veronica Mirilla Neill, daughter of Mirilla Vasiliev and the rightful heir to the throne."

After a moment of shock, the three women took a knee, bowing their heads. Adrik continued to glare at me and said something in Yazyk that I assumed was rude.

Before Pietr could answer, I held up a hand. "Here's how this is going to go. You will listen to Pietr and speak to me in the language my mother, your last tsarina, chose to teach me. Then you will follow the others' suit and take a knee or face the ramifications once I regain control of the capital. And make no mistake, I *will* bring that murderous traitor to her knees."

I took a step closer to the much bigger man, making sure he saw the fearlessness in my eyes. "You've lived long enough to recognize Mirilla's face in mine."

I wasn't going to let this man bully his way through the meeting. And if he chose to leave? His loss as far as I was concerned.

The tension in the room was tangible as he stared me down.

CHAPTER 19

Wednesday Evening

The last thing I wanted was to lose a potential ally in the battle against Galina, but there was no way in hell I would show cowardice in front of Adrik. I knew his type. He'd never follow me if I did.

With a final appraising look from head to toe, Adrik nodded. "Your mother was a good woman, a good ruler. She raised you well." He knelt before me and bowed his head.

I let out my breath as silently as possible. Okay, maybe I wouldn't dislike this man as much as I first thought. I just hoped it wouldn't be a constant fight with him—I only had the patience for one battle at a time, and even that amount was limited.

I stepped back in line with Pietr. He caught my gaze and nodded, the hint of a smile on his lips.

"As I was telling the others," he said after the others stood, "it's time to take Mirfeniksa back from the usurper. We're all in agreement that she's done too much harm to our people and land."

"Did this girl bring an army with her?" Skepticism laced Adrik's words as he eyed me.

Ugh. Keeping my cool was going to be tough.

"Once word spreads of Veronica's return, people will flock to the cause," Pietr said.

The other man sneered. "You expect us to march against Galina in the *hope* that others will join?"

My temper wasn't going to last much longer.

Mila crossed her arms over her broad yet still voluptuous chest. "It sounds as though you doubt our people."

"Not following Veronica would be a traitorous move," Feodora added. "Trust that they will join the fight."

"So, what do you propose, Pietr?" Adrik asked. "Are we to storm the palace in the dead of night? Lay siege?"

"The simple answer is yes," Pietr answered. "Whatever it takes. Once I have your agreement, plans will be drawn up and communicated via birds."

I wasn't much of a strategist, so my mind wandered as the five rebel leaders discussed battle formations and other war details. The military never appealed to me as a career choice, which wasn't a surprise to anyone who knew me. My parents gave me enough rules to follow growing up. I sure as shit wasn't going to follow anyone else's unless I had to. Even laws were negotiable.

But once we won this war, *I* would be the rule maker. What a strange turn of events.

This was such a terrible idea.

"It was a pleasure to meet you, Your Majesty," Mila's strong voice grabbed my attention.

The other phoenixes murmured their agreement and bowed. I smiled in return, even at Adrik. Kill 'em with kindness, they say. We would see how well that worked with his tough shell.

The details wrapped up for now, I followed Pietr out of the communication circle and waited until the others disappeared into the smoke.

After a quick discussion, Lena, Liz, and Ivan took their leave of the cavern. I hardly noticed, though, because a dream was about to become a reality. My heart beat frantically against my ribs, a whole mess of emotions threatening to burst forth.

It was time to meet my aunt.

Pietr nodded at Oleg, who snuffed out the flames with a blink of his eyes. He grew still again, and a new pattern emerged on the floor, forming from flames that ripped from the fireplace. Pietr held up a hand for me to wait and stepped inside the circle.

A moment later, two figures took form from the smoke. The first I had just met—Taisiya, the pint-sized younger woman who resembled the sun from head to toe. The woman beside her was taller and instantly recognizable.

"Thank you for agreeing to meet separately," Pietr said. "Until we secure the capital, anyone related to Veronica is at risk, even from the others."

Taisiya gazed up at him, her long, golden eyelashes

highlighting the bright red of her irises. "Of course, Pietr. Anything for you."

Smiling, he glanced over his shoulder at me and tilted his head.

My mouth was dry, though surprisingly not from Taisiya's obvious attraction to Haven's leader. That was only a blip on my radar and something I would consider another day.

I walked through the inferno and stared at the woman who shared my mother's face. It was almost funny. I'd worried that I wouldn't recognize her, that she wouldn't be who she claimed to be. Except I would know this woman anywhere, and my heart ached in relief as I realized I would never forget my mom's face while Zasha lived.

There were minor differences, of course. Instead of my mom's lighter strawberry strands, this woman had fiery red hair like Taisiya's. She had eyes like mine, purple instead of green. Zasha held her thin frame tall and proud like my mother had, a princess in her own right as she met my gaze at the same height. I caught the slightest bit of uncertainty and hesitation in her gaze.

Was she happy to see me, or angry that I would be taking the throne? Did she expect to be next in line?

How little I knew of this woman and her intentions for this meeting.

"Oh, my little Nica, you've returned." A genuine smile broke across her face. Her voice was warm and reminded me of family. "All grown up and looking so much like your mother."

A surprised laugh escaped my lips, and my chest burned as she used a nickname only my parents had used. "I was just thinking how much you look like she did."

Her smile wilted. "They have returned to the sun then, yes?"

I swallowed the lump. "Almost ten years ago now."

She closed her eyes and breathed deeply. "Then the usurper was getting too close."

"What do you mean?"

"Before the three of you fled, Mirilla decided that she and Dmitrei would return to the sun if Galina ever tracked them into the human world."

I bit my lip, holding in the onslaught of pain. So much secrecy, so many lies. Why hadn't they just trusted me with the truth?

"Don't take their deception personally, Nica," she said, rightfully interpreting my look. "They never wanted to keep things from you, you or your brother, but your safety was their top priority. They had a close friend in the human world, who they entrusted to look out for you and tell you everything when the time was right. No one expected you to figure it out on your own."

My nostrils flared. That close friend had to be the archangel Adam, who oversaw all Community activity in Miami. I knew it. His comment about making a promise to someone made perfect sense now. Of course he had kept this from me. Everyone always underestimated me. I'd be willing to bet he even had Community memories wiped to keep Mirognya a secret.

Wait. Maddox was born in the human world. She shouldn't have known about him.

"How do you know all of this?" I asked.

"Despite their disappearance from this world, your

mother and I remained in communication for almost two decades." Her gaze grew sorrowful. "Until she grew paranoid that the risk had grown too great."

My mom had been right to be paranoid.

"Pietr told me about Maddox's passing as well," she said softly. "Even their deaths couldn't keep you safe from her claws." She smiled again, though with a sadness that wasn't there before. "You're here now, and you look ready to take back your throne."

I gave a sheepish grin. "At least I look the part."

"More than that. Your mother got nervous before she became tsarina, and she was well-loved by her people. Now, they'll be *your* people."

I raised an eyebrow. "Are we talking about the same woman? My mom never got nervous about anything except Maddox flying."

She laughed. "Oh, do I have stories for you, dear girl."

And boy, did she. For long into the night, Zasha wove stories about their lives growing up, even about my parents falling in love. At some point, Pietr stepped out, and Taisiya faded from view. Their absence wasn't necessary, but I appreciated the show of respect and lack of distractions.

Because for a short while, my parents were alive and with me again, and I was happy.

CHAPTER 20

Thursday Morning

The day before we left for war was a frenzy of activity as everyone prepared. Warriors assessed their armor and weapons for any weaknesses, healers gathered supplies, and those staying behind ensured they had everything they'd need to survive if no one returned. It was a grim thought, but a necessary one. Despite all that, an excited chatter echoed throughout every hall and cavern.

I watched the commotion as I ate breakfast with Lena in the common area, itching to jump in and join the chaos as soon as I could.

Ivan popped up beside my seat, a mischievous twinkle in his eye. "You ready for some real fun?"

Raising an eyebrow, I scraped up the last bit of oatmeal-like food. "Depends on what that means. I'm not sure you people know what real fun is."

He whistled low. "Harsh. Come with me." He turned and headed for the ramp leading up and out of the caves.

I practically fell off my seat in my attempt to race after him. Not a very leader-like move, but only Lena was paying enough attention to laugh at me.

When we reached the surface, thick white clouds hid the sun, but the humid air wrapped itself around me like a hug from an old friend. I stood next to Ivan, reveling in the sticky sensation that most people loathed. It reminded me of Miami. For the first time since I had arrived in Mirognya, my heart didn't ache with the memory, and for once, I hadn't immediately thought of Florida as home.

"Today, we hunt," he said, grinning as my smile fell.

"I knew you guys had no idea what fun is," I moaned. "I don't have any knives on me." A fact I'd need to discuss with Pietr pronto.

"No, *moya koroleva*, today we hunt from the skies. Watch and follow my lead." He shifted into his falcon and launched into the air.

Without hesitation, I shifted forms and followed him above the trees. My spirit soared with joy. The wind rushing through my feathers was one of the best feelings in the world, especially after spending days below ground.

At first, we just flew, letting the winds take us where they willed. The breeze higher up was stronger and cooler than the last time I'd flown with Pietr, hinting at a storm to come. We drifted and dove, and I laughed inside my head.

Maddox and I had done similar dances in the sky when

he was learning to fly. I loved to tease him by gliding in close enough to brush his beak with my feathers. Gaining confidence didn't take him long, and he would turn at the last minute to knock me off balance.

Our parents hated it, always worried one of us would get hurt, but I argued that it was essential to learn how to react to surprises. Eventually, they stopped fighting me, either because they agreed, or they grew tired of trying to change my mind.

Ivan let out a screech and leveled out, his eyes scanning the trees below us. I wasn't sure what we were hunting; we weren't big enough to take down something like a deer. Not as birds, anyway.

Suddenly, he tucked his wings to his side and dove for the ground. I followed suit, letting gravity do its thing and exhilarating in the free fall.

Just as I broke through the leaves, Ivan's talons snared a fleeing rabbit. He shifted into human form mid-catch and broke the animal's neck in one sleek snap. I appreciated him not letting the animal suffer any longer than necessary.

I spread my wings and landed near him, shifting as I settled. Up close, the grey and white animal resembled a mix between a rabbit and a squirrel, with a long, puffy tail. "Nice catch. What is it?"

"A *krolka*." He thought for a moment. "There's no translation."

"Lunch?"

He shook his head. "Lena challenged us to catch thirty for those staying in Gavan."

I raised an eyebrow. "Today?"

"No." He laughed, and I sighed in relief. "This morning."

I muttered as he tucked the animal into the leather bag on his back. He handed me a similar satchel which I slung over my shoulders.

I put my hands on my hips and said, "Then let's catch thirty-one."

We high-fived and took to the skies.

By mid-morning, we'd caught five, only one of which was mine. Our lack of success quickly deflated my elation.

While I considered myself an intermediate hunter back in the human world, it had been years since I'd used my bird form as an actual means of hunting. Except for the random snack out in the ocean. Those fish were often begging me to catch them with how lazy they swam in large schools near the surface. On the other hand, these rabbit-like creatures were fast little fuckers and experts at turning and twisting mid-jump as they scattered.

After catching our seventh and my second, Ivan called for a quick rest in a shaded clearing. Back in human form, I panted against the warm air and pushed strands of wet hair off my face. He handed me a jug of water, which I gulped down greedily. As the sun rose with the day, so had the heat, and the humidity only grew thicker, stifling. Maybe this was how most people felt in Miami.

"Thirty, huh?" I slumped against a tree trunk and handed the jug back.

Ivan took a swig before pouring some over his head. "If it's any consolation, Lena's best was twenty in a whole day."

"And your best?"

"Fifteen before lunch." He practically preened with his

chest puffed out, which wasn't as nearly an effective look with his sweat and water-drenched hair.

"I'm slowing you down," I said.

"True." He tucked the water container back into his satchel. "But Lena didn't catch a single *krolka* her first time out."

I raised my eyebrows. Even I had caught two, and we still had another hour or two before lunch. "Seriously?"

"She'll probably kill me for telling you, but it'll be worth it to see her expression." He ran his hands through his wet hair, slicking it back from his face. "Ready?"

My muscles screamed in protest as I pushed myself away from the tree trunk. "If I say no, does that mean I can stay here and rest?"

"No, it just means you're a hatchling," he said.

Feigning shock, I held a hand to my chest. "Did you just call your tsarina a baby?"

He shrugged. "If the name fits."

I launched myself at him, ready to tackle and hold him until he cried for mercy. He ducked under my swing, and I caught nothing but feathers as he shifted into falcon form and swooped away. Not one to back down from a challenge, I shifted and tore after him.

When it was time to stop for lunch, we found another clearing and shifted back to human form. I was feeling pretty damn good about myself for adding two more *krolki* to our collection.

Ivan skinned one of the smaller animals with the ease of an experienced hunter while I set up a roasting stick and got a fire going. I had the easier job considering I could start a fire with a mere thought. We didn't even need a stick, not with our magic, but we did need the time to rest before we hunted again.

We got the krolki roasting, then sat back against the trees and enjoyed the peace and quiet. Relative quiet, anyway. Birds were chirping overhead, and the drone of bees, or something bee-like, provided a soothing backdrop.

"Okay, real talk," I said, unable to handle the silence any longer. "How did Pietr become the head of this whole rebellion?"

Ivan laughed. "Is it so hard to believe about him?"

"He just seems so young," I said, shrugging. "Though leading suits his personality."

"By phoenix years, he *is* young, but he's also experienced more than many." He crossed his hands behind his head. "Pietr was a captain in the royal *armiya*, the army. The military highly respects him for his accomplishments. Unfortunately, his status is also one reason he has to hide in Gavan while the others can stay in their communities."

That explained a lot. I was sure Galina would like nothing more than capturing Pietr and making an example of him. Living life in secrecy or on the run wasn't new for me, but I didn't think my experiences were anywhere close to what he'd seen.

I picked a few blades of grass and started to weave them together as I'd done as a child. "Tell me about your family."

He shrugged, but there was a slight hesitation in the movement. "Pretty normal. Mom, dad, kid sister."

"All of them were imprisoned by Galina?" I asked, adding another blade of grass to my design.

His body stilled. "How do you know about that?"

"I was sneaking out after my blow-up fight with Pietr." I grinned as Ivan whipped his head up to stare at me. "I overheard you guys talking."

He let out a short laugh and shook his head. "And you decided to stay?"

"I realized how selfish I'd behaved and wanted to make it right." My insides twisted, and I realized 'wanted' wasn't the correct word for how I felt. "*Needed* to make it right. I understand how difficult life can be without the people you love most."

He ran a hand over his face, his expression darkening. "My father was killed in one of the first rebellions before we fled. I don't even know if my mother and sister are still alive. It's been almost three years, and I haven't heard from my contact inside the palace in a few months. I fear he was discovered."

I winced. "I'm so sorry, Ivan. If only I'd known about this realm earlier. I wish my parents had trusted us with the truth."

"I don't think it was just a matter of trust," he said. "They were scared. And from what I've seen, you're a little impulsive." He grinned as I glared. "No, you're right. You're *very* impulsive."

Muttering a phoenix curse I'd learned, I paused my weaving to turn the stick holding our lunch, letting the flames cook through the meat evenly. He wasn't wrong about me.

Despite my best efforts, my thoughts turned dark. The

grass bracelet tore in my hands. "What happens if we fail to stop her, Ivan?"

"Well, first off, I don't fail at anything I do." He winked, earning a tiny pull of my cheek. Dazhbog above, he was so much like Maddox. "But in all honesty, there's no failing here. People are angry and hungry. They're watching their children starve, and they'll rise when we march. There will be no stopping our wrath. She brought this on herself."

His words were harsh but full of passion.

I just hoped he was right.

CHAPTER 21

Thursday Afternoon

Back inside the caves, Pietr met us in the main cavern at the base of the stairs leading back to my room. His expression remained neutral when he saw us. "Your aunt would like to meet with you again."

"I'll get the krolki to the storeroom," Ivan said, holding out a hand and nodding at the bag on my shoulder.

I slid the satchel off and handed it to him. "I guess you guys do know how to have a little fun around here."

He grinned and headed toward the kitchen, where another tunnel would lead to the cold storage area.

Although speaking to my aunt again filled my heart with joy, it also brought apprehension. Had something gone wrong? Was she hurt?

I followed Pietr across the common area toward the cavern we used the night before for communication. "Is everything okay?"

"She's going to help you access the powers connected to your royal bloodline," he said.

I stopped in my tracks, my mouth hanging open. Of all the things I expected him to say, *that* was not one of them. I was getting even closer to taking the throne, a fact that had slowly but surely been the cause for nervous excitement rather than pure dread.

More importantly, I knew accessing these abilities would get me even closer to my parents. I would connect with them in a way I'd never been before.

After a few more steps, Pietr must have realized I wasn't with him anymore. He came back and took my hands, an amused smile on his face. "Good surprise?"

Sweet Mokosh, he was so fucking hot when he smiled.

"You have no idea," I said.

Heat rose in my neck and face as his thumbs ran over my knuckles. My heart beat a little faster, yet ached at the same time. Why, oh why, did I have to go and fall in love with that damned reaper right before I found this world?

He squeezed my hands. "Not only are these powers your birthright, but we need everyone to know who you are without a shadow of a doubt. Having you at top fighting ability won't hurt either."

I nodded and let him lead me by the hand toward the communication cavern, still a bit in shock and caught up in my conflicting emotions. The fireplace was already blazing, and Oleg stood beside it, arms crossed over his broad chest.

Inside the circle of flames stood my aunt. Even formed from the smoke, there was no mistaking the brightness of her red hair. It fell in a braid behind her, stray wisps caressing her forehead and neck. She waited, her hands clasped in front of her in a patient stance, but her purple-hued gaze betrayed her nerves, flicking to any minor movement.

My heart swelled with love and pride. This was my family. My blood.

As I stepped through the flames, Zasha's face broke into a smile, and she held out her arms. I reached for her, except my hands went through hers like a ghostly apparition. We both laughed.

"Oh dear," she said, wiping a tear from her cheek. "You look so real. I forget you're not here."

Her happiness was contagious, and I smiled back. "I wish I was."

"Soon enough, dear girl," she said. "Now, let's awaken the rest of you, shall we?"

My stomach flip-flopped. "Let's do it."

Zasha took a deep breath and let it out, indicating I do the same. "First and foremost, relax. It isn't going to hurt, but it's going to be somewhat like a rebirth."

I wasn't sure which aspect she referred to, like the whole dying part, which could be pretty fucking painful depending on the method.

Regardless, I was in.

"Now, close your eyes," she said, and I obeyed. "Call upon your inner flame and tell it who you are. Then release it."

I peeked an eye open. "That's it?"

A smile tugged at her lips. "You were expecting more?"

"I mean, yeah," I said.

She chuckled and waved a hand at me to get on with it.

I sighed and closed my eye again. Taking a deep breath, I called on my flame. My magic rose eagerly, happy to do my bidding. I had never spoken to it directly before, and even thinking about doing so made me feel silly.

Oh well. When in Rome, right?

I am Veronica Mirilla Neill, tsarina of Mirfeniksa, I thought to the flame.

It danced within me, begging me to free it. So I did what Zasha said, and I released it.

Fire and ice raced through my limbs, and red-hot light burst from every pore of my being. Through a haze of rushing energy, I knew my body was lifting from the ground, but all sensation had fled besides shock and fascination. Everything inside of me pulled itself apart, more like teleporting than a rebirth, and I screamed. I had no idea whether the sound was only inside my head or released into the cavern, but I didn't care.

Only then did I realize that I wasn't in pain.

My DNA had pulled itself apart and rearranged some sequences, but my body was still intact. A soothing heat flushed through me as my genetic code wove itself back together.

Memories surfaced, only they weren't my own. Tears filled my eyes as I watched my mother go through a similar ceremony, then my grandmother, then her mother, and on and on. For generations, I saw the women of my family rise in their time to accept their place as protectors of their people—our people.

For the first time since I had been named tsarina, I felt

like this was right. That I could do this monumental task. Anger brewed deep within me as I thought of Galina and everything she had stolen, not just from me but from my people. We all suffered under her rule. It was time to put an end to her cruelty, to rise from the ashes of destruction left in her wake.

When solid ground formed beneath my feet again, I opened my eyes. Zasha still stood before me, only now she pressed her hands together in front of her mouth, and tears slid down her face.

"That was intense," I said.

She lowered her hands and smiled. "You're ready."

Every step after that felt like I was floating on air. My body thrummed with energy and life, and my magic was bursting at the seams. My inner flame had grown in power. It wasn't necessarily uncomfortable, but I was very aware of the difference.

As I followed Pietr back to the common area, a phoenix I didn't know yet rushed up to us. If I had to wager a guess, I'd say he was hardly out of his teens, if that.

"Pietr, uh, Your Majesty," he said in a rush. He gave a super awkward bow which made the moment even more weird.

Maybe it was the magic thrumming through my veins or the recent ancestral trip down memory lane, but I didn't mind the title or gesture this time. I wouldn't expect it of anyone, but it only drew more attention whenever I tried to stop it from happening.

"Viktor has arrived with news," he said. "He's in the war room."

Pietr and I exchanged a glance. We must have both gotten the sense it wouldn't be good news. Changing direction, we headed to the stairs leading up to the war room.

"Who's Viktor?" I asked as we climbed.

"One of our palace scouts," Pietr said. "He's a footman and among the first to greet visitors."

I hadn't realized we had more than one phoenix on the inside. "Isn't that dangerous?"

"Very." Pietr's jaw clenched. "He refuses to leave his post, knowing how invaluable his information is to us."

Lena and Ivan had already gathered at the stone table inside the war room, along with a phoenix I assumed was Viktor. His long hair was the color of starlight—as white as white could be—and pulled into a half-ponytail. Matching eyebrows sat above light-yellow eyes, and his skin was pale but not nearly as white as his hair.

All three stood and bowed.

I faced Viktor, meeting his strange gaze. "Thank you for continuing to aid the cause despite the incredible risk to your life."

"It is my duty and honor, Your Majesty." His voice was light and airy, almost matching his unique coloring.

"What's happened?" Pietr asked.

"The fae mages reached the capital a couple of days ago," Viktor said. "This morning, her five best hunters departed."

Pietr's shoulders sagged. "She knows."

Fuck.

I clenched my fists at my sides. Keeping Galina in the dark about me for as long as possible had been our modus operandi, but I hadn't planned on William fucking everything up once again. I should have known better.

Our plan had just become a race against time.

CHAPTER 22

Thursday Evening

Dinner in the war room that night wasn't the jovial affair most of the others had been. Tensions were high, and everyone was feeling it.

Lena and Ivan had their heads close together, heatedly discussing weapon choices. Across from me, Liz was as quiet as I was. She wouldn't be fighting, but her job would be almost more difficult. Witnessing the atrocities and consequences of war as she attempted to save lives and limbs. Over her head, Oleg and Pavel argued about various strategies for getting inside the palace.

I idly picked at my plate, nowhere near hungry but knowing my body was going to need the fuel to get through the next few days. I might have prepared my whole life to fight, but I'd never led an army into actual war before. People were going to die—a *lot* of people on both sides. I swallowed hard. Good people and those who had been misguided. Of course, there'd be some in there who deserved death, like Galina and William.

The fork shook in my hand as I tightened my grip. Oh, I would enjoy their deaths very much.

Pietr leaned forward to rest his arms on the table beside his plate, his food hardly touched. "Since none of us seems to be interested in eating tonight, let's discuss tomorrow. We can strike even harder now, no secrecy necessary."

Pavel let out a whoop of excitement, making most of us smile. Liz's face was still deep in thought, her eyebrows furrowed. I wondered if she was remembering her parents. Whether she witnessed them die or not, it was an experience that must have scarred her deeply. Or maybe she was envisioning the accumulation of the dying and dead. Either way, I wanted to reach out and ease the pain of those memories.

"In the morning, we move out," Pietr continued. "The griffins arrived a short while ago and will receive their cargo at dawn. Due to the distance, we'll fly in a V-shaped formation in teams of nine. We'll spread out, launching at various intervals until we stop for the evening. You've trained your teams for years. Now we get to put that training into action.

"Tonight, we'll do our best to let it all go until tomorrow," he said. "Let's meet at the hot spring in one hour for our traditional soak."

I raised an eyebrow, my cheeks twitching with barely

contained amusement. "You guys take a bath together before a fight?"

Smiling, Pietr pushed his chair back to stand, and my heart gave a little flutter of excitement. He was a gorgeous specimen of a man.

He winked. "Might as well take advantage of living in a cave with a hot spring, right?"

"Oh, definitely." I tried not to focus too much on the way his muscular body moved with such grace as he turned to leave. His sculpted backside was an even better view.

Was it getting warm in here?

An image of Thane's smoldering smirk snuck into my mind, as well as the memory of a heat that could never be replicated. Before they hurt too much, I pushed those thoughts away.

An hour passed much too quickly, but I was excited to partake in the so-called traditional soak. I'd never turn down the chance for a hot bath. Add in some good company, and it sounded like trouble waiting to happen. Maybe that was the goal—a little tension reliever before the big day.

Come to think of it, if I was walking into an orgy, I was naiver than I thought. But I also wasn't going to say no. The more I thought about it, orgies before battle might be the reason my parents never told me about this place. Unlikely, but possible.

As usual, Pavel waited for me outside my door. After dinner, we had stuck around for idle chit chat until everyone dispersed. He'd accompanied me back to my room, standing guard outside while I changed into the closest thing I had to swimwear. I hoped I wasn't the only one who would be showing up in a tank top and underwear, at any rate. I threw on the robe I had acquired at some point and opened the door.

"So, tell me," I said as we walked down the hallway to the stairs, "Is this an actual tradition, or am I being lured into an orgy?"

Pavel's deep red eyes widened, then he threw his head back to laugh. "Does it matter if you're coming along eager and willing? Or even just willing?"

I shrugged. "Hey, we're all consenting adults, right?"

"Sadly, there won't be an orgy tonight." He paused for a moment just before we reached the turn in the corridor leading to the stairs. "I don't think so, anyway."

"I'm not sure whether I'm relieved or hurt," I said, holding back a laugh.

Before we stepped into view of the common area, he caught my arm and grinned down at me. "You know, there's more than a few of us who would be willing to scratch any itches you may have. No strings attached unless that's what you wanted."

Pavel wasn't lacking in the looks department, and I'd be lying if I hadn't eyed him a time or two in the way he suggested. But I had enough confusion going on in my mind and heart between Thane and Pietr. I didn't need to add any more problems to my cluttered plate of emotions.

"I'll keep that in mind." I winked at him and headed down the stairs, pretending not to hear his playful muttering behind me.

The hour was late, which meant the main cavern was empty save for a few people cleaning up after the hectic day of preparation. Everyone else was getting much-needed rest before the war.

As we approached the steam-filled hall leading into the bath, laughter and voices trickled out to meet us. We must have been the last to arrive.

Turned out I was right.

Already inside the circular pool, Ivan and Lena were taking turns seeing who could squirt water the farthest from their cupped hands. Oleg and Liz were pretending not to notice each other too much, speaking quietly while sitting side by side on the underwater bench. Even Pietr was there, relaxing with his back against the side, his arms stretched out on top and an amused smile on his lips.

"There you are!" Lena shouted and splashed water in our direction.

"It's hardly been an hour." I hung up my robe and dropped into the pool. The burn felt beyond amazing on my sore muscles.

"Turns out we're all too impatient." Ivan held up his wrinkled palms.

I laughed and drifted over to an open spot against the side wall near Pietr. "Is soaking before battle a tradition just for this small group?"

"Ivan and Pavel started it." Lena grinned. "Neither wanted to admit they love a good long soak, so it became a new 'tradition' instead."

Ivan shrugged. "I had to get you all to bathe somehow."

Lena growled and splashed water hard in his direction. He dipped below the surface only to drag her down squealing until she submerged.

I laughed along with the others. The more I saw the two of them together, the more they displayed a brother-sister type relationship, rather than romantic like I first thought. Ivan might have been more like Maddox than I realized, preferring men to women. I actually had no idea whether or not there was a gay community in Mirfeniksa.

Although my parents had been super supportive of Maddox, they always pushed me hard to find a partner and make babies. Now I knew that was likely due to my secret royal lineage.

"That's it for me tonight," Liz said, climbing out and wrapping herself in a towel. "I'm turning into mush. See you all in the morning."

Oleg followed only a moment later, a move that Ivan and Lena found immensely amusing. Except they didn't stay long either, and Pavel also excused himself, citing a need for a late-night snack. I'd noticed that he was one of those types that ate everything in sight and never seemed to gain a pound. Lucky bastard. The three phoenixes headed down the corridor, their words and laughter echoing back toward us.

And just like that, I was alone with Pietr. A nearly naked Pietr with the body of a demi-god.

Fucking hell.

"So, have you ever gone to war before?" I was terrible with awkward silences.

He chuckled, the sound a deep rumble in his chest. "Not like this, no. We've had skirmishes with the dragons and merfolk in the distant past. There's also a phoenix clan to the southeast that claims to be free from anyone's rule but tries to make trouble from time to time."

That was almost hard to believe. "Galina lets them live free?"

"More like they're not worth the effort," he said.

I nodded, doing my best to keep my gaze from wandering the hard lines of his arms and shoulders. Talk about effort. We were sitting much too close for comfort now that everyone had left. Warm water ran down my neck. Or maybe it was nervous sweat.

"Listen, Pietr—" I stopped when I met his gaze, my breath catching in my throat. His rainbow eyes smoldered darkly with desire as his gaze drifted over my face.

He wanted me.

Before I knew what I was doing, I reached a hand toward him. My fingers brushed his cheek, and I traced my thumb across his lips. They were so full and soft, such a contrast to the rest of his body.

What better way to forget the past than trying something new?

Big hands encircled my waist and pulled me onto his lap, the hot water sloshing around us. He drew my mouth to him with a firm hand at the back of my neck.

Moaning against his lips, I crushed my body against him, curling my arms around his shoulders. Every inch of his hardened muscles was taut beneath my hands. Our tongues entwined, dancing together eagerly.

I wanted more.

Sucking his lower lip into my mouth, I earned a deep-throated growl. The sound rumbled through our mouths and down to the lowest part of my belly, warming me even further.

His free hand gripped my hip and pulled me closer. The hardness of his arousal rubbed against me. Gasping, I dropped my head back as waves of desire swept through me. His other hand tightened to a fist in my hair, pulling my head farther back. My exposed neck was easy prey for his mouth as he descended on me.

I wanted him inside me, right here, right now, thrusting hard and deep, making me forget everything else.

His lips and tongue moved along the sensitive skin of my neck to my clavicle. Gripping his shoulders, I dug my nails into his skin, relieving some of the tension eating up my body. He growled again, sending shock waves through to my core.

His hand left my hip and dove between my legs. The palm of his hand rubbed against me, teasing my swollen clit before he slipped a finger beneath my panties and straight inside me.

It had been way too long since my last orgasm, and I was most definitely not going to last long.

As I thrust against his hand, his grip on my hair loosened and moved to support my back. Moaning in ecstasy, I let my head fall backward again. His tongue found my nipple through my tank top, drawing it into his mouth, fabric and all. I whimpered, and he slipped a second finger inside me.

As expected, I didn't last. Only a few strokes later, my body spasmed around his fingers, claiming them in the throes of release I had desperately needed. He continued to swirl his tongue around my nipple as I rode the orgasmic wave to completion, every part of me shuddering from aftershocks.

Holy shit, that felt good.

He withdrew his fingers and moved his hand back to my hip, gripping my skin tight enough to earn another whimper. Not of pain, but wanting more. Wanting him deeper inside me.

Our gazes locked together, and I knew he wanted the same. I reached down into the water and freed his cock. Taking him in my palm, I stroked his hard length. He was thick, and his groans of pleasure as I applied more pressure only encouraged me.

But I couldn't wait any longer.

I brought him closer, ready to receive him fully. I wanted to ride him until we both came—again and again.

A sharp pain lanced through the left side of my chest, just above my boob. I cried out, releasing Pietr to press my hands against my chest.

"What happened?" he asked, his voice gruff with desire but tinted with concern.

The pain was too intense to speak. I squeezed my eyes shut and tried to breathe through the stabs. He pulled my hands from my chest and slid my wet top down my left shoulder. The red mark that had been growing above my boob pulsed angrily.

Pietr looked up at me sharply, shock and anger replacing the desire in his eyes. "You've chosen a mate?"

Was I hearing things, or did this man just ask me if I had chosen a mate like I was some godsdamned animal? "Not that it's any of your business, but I haven't had sex in way too fucking long. I don't know what the fuck this thing is, but it hurts like hell right now."

As if in response, the mark pulsed again, making me wince.

Pietr's grip on my hips eased, but anger still rippled beneath the surface of his face. "That *thing* is a bonding mark. Once a phoenix's flame has chosen a worthy mate, they're bonded for life."

I stared at him as if he'd just sprouted a third eye. "That's literally impossible in my case."

"Why?"

"Because the only other person I've had feelings for is dead," I said.

Pietr blinked at me.

"He's a grim reaper. Or was. He's probably getting his angel wings as we speak." My heart ached in time with the pulsing mark the more I thought of Thane. "Besides, what does that have to do with us right now?"

Pietr sighed and moved me off his lap to sit beside him. "As long as your mate walks the earth, your body will reject any attempts to mate with another."

"You have *got* to be kidding me." I was so close to finally getting a good deep dicking, and my body had to go and betray me.

Why the fuck had it even chosen the reaper?

I couldn't have a future with Thane, only a few soul-shattering lays before he was off to angel la la land. And if he were already an angel, then I wouldn't get that much. Either scenario, I'd be left a heartbroken mess, even if the time spent with him was worth it.

This man right here was a prize specimen of my own kind. He could give me everything I wanted and more, and my body shut that shit down. Friend-zoned him against my will.

Did this mean I'd never get to have sex again?

What kind of a broken mate-picker did I have?

CHAPTER 23

Thursday Evening

I put my hands over my face, not quite sure how I felt about this situation with Pietr anymore. I needed to be alone for a moment to process. Come to think of it, I didn't know how I felt about anything right about now. Life had just thrown me a huge fucking curveball.

Was I going to be alone for the rest of my life? And what did that mean for the future of the royal family? Or for Mirfeniksa?

A warm, reassuring hand rested on my shoulder. "Veronica, look at me."

Dropping my hands, I met Pietr's gaze. His anger had dissipated into something more like calm acceptance. Or maybe it was disappointment. I was still terrible at reading people, especially those who were so good at hiding their emotions in the first place.

He took one of my hands in his and sighed. "When this battle is over, I'm going to help you get home to him."

"There's no point except to say goodbye." My lungs constricted with the realization that I was destined to be alone. Pietr's kindness only made it worse.

"Then you'll say goodbye," he said firmly. "And after, your flame will decide whether or not it wants to break the bond."

I wasn't sure if I heard him right. "Wait, you said this mark bonded us for life."

"Correct, but I don't know what happens if one half of the bond becomes an angel." He gave me a strained smile. "It's been centuries since anyone's created a bond outside the phoenix species. Certainly not with someone who's already died."

I sighed. "Apparently I have a knack for shaking up the status quo."

"Indeed." His gaze turned distant, and I took that moment of quiet to process my thoughts.

If I was candid with myself, I didn't feel the same way toward Pietr that I did Thane, even though I really, *really* wanted to. Sure, I had an intense attraction to the phoenix rebel—who wouldn't?—but it wasn't the destiny-defying connection that I'd always felt toward the reaper. I was pretty sure I would never feel that way again.

I blinked away the moisture forming in my eyes. "I'm sorry."

Pietr shook his head. "Don't be. I'm thankful to have

you in my life, no matter the role. You're an amazing woman, Veronica. If there's even the smallest chance of completing your mate bond, then I want to help you do it."

"Well, shit." I gave a quick laugh, the sound breaking with a half sob. "I was trying not to cry."

With a final smile, Pietr pulled himself out of the pool and grabbed a towel. "Stay and relax, *moya koroleva*. We'll start fresh tomorrow."

I watched his dripping wet back exit through the tunnel, wishing for all the world that he was right. That bonding with a man destined for the heavens would free me once he ascended.

Otherwise, I was looking at a few centuries of loneliness.

Something nagged at the back of my mind all night, making me toss and turn and get the worst night's sleep since I'd first arrived in Haven. Back then, I had the fever to blame, but now I had a feeling that there was more to this whole bonded mate mark thing.

A piece of the puzzle was missing.

When I finally gave up on drifting back to sleep, I threw on some clothes, then hurried through the corridors. My two guards worked hard to keep up with me. I burst into the cavern used for communicating with the other rebel leaders. Pietr and Oleg looked over from the fireplace, and Pietr's face immediately grew concerned.

"Is everything okay?" he asked.

"Honestly, I don't know," I said, out of breath from the rush over. "I need to know something about the mark. The mate one."

Oleg's eyebrows drew up, but he stayed as silent as ever.

"Does this need to be a private discussion?" Pietr asked, glancing at the guards behind me.

"No. I mean, I don't care," I said, waving a hand to dismiss the question. I should probably care more about keeping it between us, but I was too anxious. "I keep coming back to this idea that my flame might decide to let the bond go once Thane ascends. But it hasn't yet, and we know that because I still have the damn mark. Does that mean he hasn't ascended yet? He's still… him?"

Pietr placed his hands on my shoulders just as I was about to start pacing. "I don't know. While that sounds like a logical answer, we just don't have the history to know for sure."

I chewed on my bottom lip. I had to be right; deep down in my soul, I knew that Thane was still with me. As the reaper, as in *not* an angel. Which meant I needed to get back to Miami as soon as possible. I had even more of a reason to get this show on the road.

"When do we leave for the capital?" I asked.

Releasing my shoulders, Pietr smiled, though it held a hint of sadness. I hadn't forgotten our steamy moment the night before, not by a long shot, but I was grateful that things weren't awkward between us today. He was too good of a man to let that happen.

"Within the hour," he said. "Oleg and I are confirming the other leaders are ready to move out. We also need to let them know that the secret of your identity has been compromised. It's not quite a surprise attack when the other party knows you're coming."

I nodded and turned to go.

"Why don't you stay and listen?" Oleg's calm voice caught me off guard. I'd rarely heard the big man speak, but his voice was always as smooth as a newborn baby's butt, no matter how weird that sounded. "It would do you good to learn more about the others, especially when they don't know you're here."

I grinned up at him. Who knew he had a devious side to him? "I like the way you think."

While I stood to the side, Oleg closed his eyes and did his thing, which looked like absolutely nothing. This time I knew better.

When the fire leaped from the fireplace and the communication circle roared to life, Pietr stepped inside. The other leaders' shadowy forms soon joined him— Taisiya, Feodora, and Mila.

Everyone except Adrik.

My skin prickled with apprehension the longer we waited. Had he changed his mind about joining us? Or even worse, had he switched sides?

Pietr's shoulders slumped slightly. "I feared Adrik would abandon us when the time came, but I had hoped he would prove me false. Regardless, it's time, my friends."

"We are with you, Pietr," Feodora said, her deep blue eyes blazing with pride. Today, she wore her dark brown hair long and loose, and the streaks of white glittered in the firelight. "You and our true tsarina."

The other two women nodded their heads in his direction, standing straighter and taller—as much as anyone could consider tiny Taisiya tall, anyway.

"Her Majesty is lucky to have such loyalty from Mirfeniksa's fiercest leaders," he said. "Unfortunately, Galina has become aware of Veronica's arrival and our subsequent attack."

Mila swore under her breath, and the other two women grumbled.

"The mages?" Taisiya asked.

He nodded. "Regardless, Gavan moves out within the hour."

"Well, we have some good news," Mila said, the leathery wrinkles at the corners of her mouth and eyes growing even deeper with a grim smile.

Though she was of the same height as Feodora, she was also twice as wide. The broadsword strapped to her back and the multitude of thick, angry scars traversing her arms added to her overall ferocity. She was a woman not to be messed with. "The smaller towns have been sending their warriors to join the march. People cheer Veronica's name."

My ears blazed with heat. I didn't feel like I deserved anyone's cheers, but I was also super excited to know people were rallying to the cause, to bring Galina to her knees. If I was the catalyst, then so be it.

"Unfortunately, there is some more bad news as well," she continued. "Galina is doing her best to discredit Veronica, calling her an imposter to those who will listen. Those within reach of her spell are impatient for the fight."

Pietr nodded. "I expected that. What of the fae and human mages who arrived in the capital? Any word?"

"Galina would have them by her side, heavily protected," Taisiya spoke up, her curly red hair as wild as her eyes. She might be smaller than the others and most people in general, but no one would overlook this woman. "We haven't been able to determine what their arrangement is yet."

"Keep digging," he said. "If their magic can help her in any way, we need to stop it quickly. Our people will die today—a true death. I do not doubt that Galina will encourage her soldiers to use their flames against us. We must be ready to do the same."

The three women shared a knowing glance before nodding. "We are prepared, Pietr."

"And what of Adrik?" Taisiya asked, placing her hands on her hips. "Will he be held accountable if he fails to prove his loyalty to the crown?"

Pietr spread his hands. "That will be up to our tsarina."

The small woman grumbled but didn't argue.

"Let us move out." He kissed his fist and raised it toward the ceiling. "May Mother Mokosh guide us home."

As the women copied his gesture and words, goosebumps raced up my arms. The prayer was a blessing to keep our trip safe as we returned to the capital.

It was also a blessing on the soul should we fall beneath another phoenix's fiery blade, never to rise again.

According to Ivan, flying to the capital would take us most of the day and some of the next. Sokol wasn't far in the grand scheme of things, but speed slows significantly when you're moving an entire army.

I followed Pietr out of the caves and through the vines covering the main entrance. A cool breeze teased my hair back from my neck. I'd expected the sun to warm my skin this morning, but angry dark clouds obscured the sky.

"Figures a storm would be brewing," Ivan said, popping up at my side, Lena right behind him. "The only question is who the gods are rooting for."

"You don't think it's for us?" I asked.

Ivan's eyes scanned the rolling clouds. "I don't pretend to know what the gods are thinking."

"That's such a lie." Lena flicked his ear lobe. "You already started a betting pool that the storm will hold off until we reach the capital. Even though the elders suggested we get ready for a muddy sleep tonight."

He grinned. "Just a friendly wager."

"And how well off will you be if you're right?" she asked.

Letting the two continue their bickering, I took in the scene before us. Warriors were saying goodbye, hugging loved ones, and tickling babies and children until they laughed. Should the worst occur, their families would remember the smiles and bittersweet happiness of this day.

As much as I wanted to tear my gaze away and not focus on the heartbreak, I made myself watch. These people were putting their lives on the line because their tsarina had returned—me of all people. The least I could do was share their pain.

A weird grunting came from my right, and I gasped when I saw what made the noise. Was that what I thought it was?

Griffins.

Five of them. The massive creatures' back halves were all lions, covered in short, tawny-colored fur that revealed powerful haunches and legs. Their front halves were eagles. From dark brown wings tucked tight against their bodies to deadly talons and sharp beaks, all of which were as long as my hand.

Phoenixes adjusted the animals' harnesses and loaded up the giant wagons. The tallest phoenix caring for the beasts only came up to their shoulders, and he was by no means short.

One of the griffins turned to look straight at me, and I gulped down a wave of fear.

"Beautiful, aren't they?" Pietr's voice at my side made me jump.

"Incredible." Definitely an understatement, but I didn't know how else to describe them and how they made me feel. Vulnerable, yet oddly safe.

"Would you like to meet them?" he asked.

"Like, get close to those talons that could rip us apart in a heartbeat?"

"They're harmless unless provoked." He took my hand. "Come on."

I didn't want to be rude by not going but damn if my heart didn't want to jump right out of my chest. The smell of oiled leather mixed with something sweet, like honey, and tickled my nose.

All five griffins turned to face me as we approached. I definitely would have noped right out of that meeting had Pietr not been dragging me along.

My last encounter with a beast larger than myself ended with a hole in my shoulder and near death. And that was only a manticore, puny compared to these creatures. I knew my limits.

To make matters worse, the one closest to us took a step forward and chirped. Its head tilted to the side as if in question. The others moved closer as well, disregarding the shouts from their handlers.

Not ready to be eaten today, I was about to turn and run except, as one, the griffins bowed their heads before me.

"Your Majesty," said one of the handlers who came running up. He offered a quick bow. "I didn't see you coming. At least Mudryy recognized you. He knew your mother and father well."

I swallowed to wet my suddenly dry mouth. "They're beautiful."

The five griffins straightened their necks and ruffled their feathers. I shot a curious glance at Pietr.

"Yes, they can understand you." He stepped forward and ran a hand down the closest eagle's neck. Mudryy leaned into his touch, resting his head on Pietr's shoulder. Vivid yellow eyes remained fixed on me. "Handlers are taught from a young age to interpret the griffins' calls and movements to ensure their needs are met."

I shook my head, as much from disbelief as amazement. "I'm not sure how to come to terms with the idea you keep griffins as pets."

The eagle's head whipped off Pietr's shoulder. Glare was probably the best word for the look the bird was giving me now. Mudryy stalked forward menacingly, his talons digging into the dirt with each step. Lowering his head, he tilted it to the side to look me straight in the eye.

I gulped. "I'm assuming you don't like being called a pet."

The giant bird blinked and dipped its head.

"My apologies, Mudryy," I stammered. "I'm new at all this."

Something cold slipped into my hand, and I glanced down to find a vegetable of some sort. Orange and oblong, like a weird carrot or potato. Pietr winked at me and stepped back. I held the food out toward the griffin.

With a whistle and lightning-fast move, the vegetable was gone, and the griffin was munching happily. The animal plodded back toward the others. With complete certainty, I knew it could have taken my fingers, or even a whole fist, just as quickly.

I let out a slow breath. A heavy hand fell on my shoulder, startling me. Pietr smiled down at me.

"What?" I asked.

"They'll follow you to the ends of the earth now," he said.

I raised an eyebrow. "For giving one a snack?"

"They can sense who you are."

The griffins preened and ruffled their feathers as their handlers loaded the last of our goods.

"And just like that, they'll follow me?" I asked.

"Just like that." The warmth in Pietr's voice reassured me.

If only everyone else would be so easily convinced.

CHAPTER 24

Friday Morning

Within an hour of meeting the griffins, Pietr had our small army airborne and headed toward Sokol, the capital. Even better, he'd finally given me back my knives, plus a few extra.

I'd tucked them into every crevice of my armor that I could fit them without stabbing myself. A sword hung sheathed on my hip. The blade wasn't Lisa, my trusty short sword named for the Russian word for she-fox, but it would do in a pinch.

I was armed and dangerous and ready to kick some ass.

The air rushing beneath my wings was cool and crisp, hinting at the impending storm. With any luck for us—and for Ivan's bet—we'd make camp for the night before the rain started. I had more than enough turbulence going on in my mind; I didn't need a soggy butt to make it worse.

Each flap of my wings left me wondering if this would be our last flight. I had killed others before, and I knew the emotional toll it took, no matter the reason or justification for the death. Some of these warriors were seasoned fighters, and I was sure there were those among them who had far more kills than I did.

But I knew for a fact that many with us had never been in a real fight, had never seen blood spurting from a mortal wound. A wound that *they* had caused. A life they had taken. If we came out of this mess alive and victorious, would we find ourselves somehow changed?

And if we failed, what would Galina do to those she captured, the people I befriended and even came to love as family?

Try as I might not to, my thoughts constantly returned to Thane. I wished he was here by my side, ready to fight with me. He would have, too, if he had been able to join me. You know, if I hadn't leaped through a portal after a megalomaniac fae.

Except if I hadn't, I would have never found Maddox's true killer and my rightful place in the world. I still wasn't completely sold on that last part, but I would see how I felt after dethroning Galina.

As we flew into a dark grey cloud bank, our visibility became almost non-existent. It wasn't a problem, though. We knew our formation and kept the pace steady.

Something flew into me, knocking me feet over beak. A set of talons sank into my feathers, catching skin and pulling me down.

I twisted to peck at my captor, only to find another set of talons clutching my neck. We plummeted out of the clouds, my stomach in my throat as we rushed toward the forest below.

Held as tightly as I was, I hit the ground hard. My breath whooshed out, and my bones protested painfully. I shifted into human form and struggled against whoever held me. Like a cornered animal, fear and fury ripped through me. I bit down hard on an arm that came within reach.

A shout of pain identified one of my captors as male, and the hands loosened enough for me to wrench free. I whipped around, knives in hand, to face my attackers.

Two male phoenixes circled me, swords raised and features obscured by dark masks and cloaks. Only their hardened eyes were visible, laser-focused on their target—me.

Except something was wrong with their eyes. There was no color, no shade except pitch black, like their pupils encompassed everything else.

No phoenix should have eyes like that.

The blades they held lit up with fire. The kind of fire that would earn me a one-way introduction to the gods. Dread mixed with cold certainty in the pit of my stomach.

This was a take no prisoners kind of a deal. I had no way of knowing if these hunters were under Galina's spell or following her orders because they chose to. Either way, I wasn't going down without a fight. Thank the gods Pietr convinced me to put on armor before our flight.

They attacked at the same time.

I blocked both their strikes, dancing out of the way as I slashed back. Fire singed my cheek—a narrow miss from one of their follow-up swings that nearly connected with my throat. I hissed against the pain. The phoenix fire itself wouldn't kill me, but a stab in the right place sure would. I faced them again.

"You realize you're fighting for a fraud, right?" I stepped forward and jabbed, forcing one of them to block. Ducking under the other one's attack, I threw myself to the side and rolled. I jumped to my feet and circled them. "Why are you doing this?"

Neither of them replied, only stared at me with those creepy black eyes.

Before they could attack again, I threw one of my knives along with a rope of fire. The phoenix I aimed at deflected the blade, but my whip-like flame coiled itself around his neck and tightened. He pulled at the binding, only to find it still wrapped around him, all the way down his legs. The flaming rope cinched tighter, knocking him off his feet. He fell with a grunt.

The guy still standing rushed me, but a flurry of wings and talons descended on him as a squadron of phoenixes arrived and forced him to the ground.

Pietr shifted into human form and strode toward me, his eyes full of concern. "Are you hurt?"

"Physically, I'm peachy." The aches in my bones and scratch across my cheek would soon heal. I looked at my would-be murderers, an unsettled feeling remaining in my stomach. "They intended to kill, but I don't think they're all there if you know what I mean. Their eyes are completely black."

"Galina's magic," he said, his expression grim. "I wish we knew what it was. It's hard to fight back when we've never seen its kind before."

That didn't sound promising. "How are we going to win then?"

"She's not invincible," he said. "No one is. Our numbers and fury will best her, no matter how dark her magic. Light will always banish the shadows, and our fire is nothing if not pure light."

I wanted to believe it as strongly as he did, but doubts riddled my thoughts. I'd encountered many different types of magic in the human world, from the witches to the fae. Nothing I'd seen matched this.

All I could do was hope that he was right.

A griffin landed nearby while the other phoenixes worked to bind the attackers with flame-retardant handcuffs and chains. They were then thrown unceremoniously across and strapped to the griffin's back. Not only would the bindings withstand phoenix fire, but they would also prevent the men from shifting and flying away.

I guess I learned a thing or two from those books after all.

"Are you okay to fly?" Pietr asked.

I nodded, but I remained focused on the attackers. "What will happen to them?"

"We'll hold them until the war is won," he said. "If her magic has corrupted them, they'll be freed when she falls. We'll question them and determine their allegiance to the true crown."

"And if they're not freed?" I asked.

He glanced over his shoulder at the two phoenixes. "If they prove to be loyal to the usurper even after her death, then they will face their justice before the gods."

A harsh but fair fate.

CHAPTER 25

Friday Evening

When Pietr finally called a halt to our flight that evening, I was beyond exhausted. My entire body quivered in protest on two legs. It wasn't so much the physical exertion of flying and fighting, so much as the mental and emotional toll.

Galina's hunters had tracked me down and tried to kill me. As in final death kind of kill, never to rise again. I'd never been so close to actual death before. Not my own, anyway.

As we made our camp for the night, I refused to let anyone do anything for me that I could do myself. A stubbornness I started to regret halfway into pitching my tent.

My parents took Mad and me camping a few times and made sure we knew how to set up a shelter, but that was using modern tent-making tools and the internet as a guide. This random-pieces-of-sticks set didn't come with click-together parts, and it sure as shit didn't have instructions.

At least the rain hadn't started yet. Ivan must have been happy about that.

Muttering under my breath, I didn't hear anyone approach until a finger tapped me on the shoulder. Hands on her hips, Lena surveyed the mess I had made.

"Need some help?" she asked with laughter in her voice.

"I swear I know how to do this with a human tent," I grumbled. "The kind with poles that snap together and bend on their own."

She grinned. "Your only problem here is not using your flame to bend the wood."

"Because wood catches fire…" Sometimes I cringed at the things that came out of my mouth.

She rolled her eyes and picked up one of the sticks. "I didn't say use *all* of your flame."

Holding the stick out in front of her, Lena ran her other hand along the length of it, a red glow following in her palm's wake. Once the entire stick was glowing, she bent it with her hands.

"Why do you have to make it look so easy?" I took the stick from her and tied it to another with a piece of twine.

With Lena's help, I finished my tent and prayed the gusts wouldn't knock it down. Night had fallen while we worked, and with the storm threatening to unleash its fury at any moment, not a star peeped through the leafy canopies above us.

At long last, we joined the others around the campfire for a well-deserved dinner. I was pretty sure we were the last of our group to arrive, thanks to my lack of camping skills.

We ate in silence, all of us casting anxious glances at the sky, hoping we would get through the meal without getting rained out. Our dinner might not have been a gourmet event like my date with Colin at The Bazaar, but the meaning behind it was so much more real. We were on our way to unseat the usurper, a violent criminal who had more than earned her death.

I took a bite of food and chewed. Wow. I hadn't thought of Colin once since arriving in Mirognya. Only a few short weeks ago, I'd considered dating the attractive fae man.

While I was just as single now as I was then, too much had happened for me to view Colin as a potential suitor. I still didn't fully know where his loyalties lay, but at least he had shown up at the end of the fight against William in Miami.

Too bad about Kit's magic nearly crucifying him.

"V, you still with us?" Pavel's voice interrupted my memories.

I raised my gaze. Everyone was staring at me as if waiting for a response. I smiled sheepishly. "I guess I got lost for a moment."

Lena snickered. "Longer than a moment."

"To be honest, I'm exhausted. I think I'll call it an early night." I stood and dusted off the seat of my pants.

Thankfully, no one argued against it. With a quick wave, I headed for my tent.

Lena caught up to me. "Do you want me to paint you?"

Was this some sort of Titanic movie reference? "I'm sorry, what?"

"War paint," she said, dispelling my confused thoughts. She tilted her head toward her tent. "It'll help separate our troops from theirs. Not that we need it, but it's tradition. Since it's your first war here, I can show you how we apply it. The others will do their own."

Sleep was a tempting thought, but war paint piqued my interest more. I followed her inside and sat cross-legged on a rug where she indicated. "It's my first war period. Facing the necromancers in Miami was nothing compared to this."

Grinning, Lena collected some supplies from her bag. "This one's gonna be epic."

"Aren't you scared?" I asked as she sat across from me and laid out the paints and brushes. Her enthusiasm wasn't entirely unexpected.

"Of course. I'd be stupid not to be, but I'm more scared about what will happen if we don't stop her." She opened one of the paints, a pale lilac, and dipped a thin brush in. "Galina has taken something from everyone, whether it be their loved ones, homes, or freedom. Now, close your eyes and hold still."

I did as told, and cold wetness touched my face. From time to time, Lena would lean close enough for her breath to tickle my skin before she moved on to a new design. The exercise provided the perfect time to mull over everything she said and mentally prepare myself for tomorrow.

Whether we won or lost, I was proud to be among those fighting for a better life. No one deserved to live the way Galina had forced them. No one deserved to see their parents' heads on a spike as Lena and Liz had. It was atrocious. Inhumane.

The soft strokes continued to sweep across my face, lulling me into a sort of meditative trance. I wondered what life would be like here on a day-to-day basis as the tsarina. I wasn't sure I'd ever really get used to the idea, but I was willing to try. *After* I got the chance to say goodbye to Thane and Kit.

Although, I didn't have to say a forever goodbye to Kit. Once Galina was gone, I would open the portals between worlds and allow everyone to come and go as they pleased.

Who knew? Maybe Kit and Angela could even summer at the palace. My cheeks twitched as I attempted to hold in a smile.

"Quit," Lena said. "You're going to smudge that one."

"Sorry." I barely moved my lips.

"What's so funny?"

I hummed my response to make it clear that speaking would be just as disastrous to the design as smiling. She muttered something in Yazyk that I was sure wasn't pleasant and resumed her painting.

"There." Her warm closeness faded. "You can look now."

I opened my eyes and accepted the offered mirror. Purple paint swept along my cheekbones in dancing flame patterns, the brush strokes becoming feathery in their design and lightness as they neared my temples. The color was faint, not quite as vibrant as I expected for war paint.

It was perfect.

"It's beautiful," I murmured, not wanting to move my lips. "Thank you."

"Don't worry about smudging it now," she said. "I added a quick-drying, waterproof agent. That bad boy will be on there for a few days no matter how hard you scrub."

That would have been nice to know first. Oh well, everyone else would have theirs, too.

"I also have stuff that'll take it off as soon as you're ready," she said as she put away her supplies.

A strange realization settled over me. I took her hands. "Thank you for being my friend, Yelena. I didn't have many growing up, and I still don't. You have no idea what it means to me."

She winked and squeezed my hands. "Just don't forget about me when you're sitting pretty on your throne, all covered in jewels and dealing with more important things." She paused. "Just don't ever call me Yelena again."

"Never," I said and meant it.

CHAPTER 26

Saturday Morning

Just before dawn, we packed up camp and headed for the capital on foot. Spending most of my twenties as a night owl, I normally would have complained about the early wakeup. Except I'd hardly slept at all, and from the look of some of the others, I wasn't the only one.

The city of Sokol wasn't far now, and if everything else went as planned, then we would be among the last to arrive. Galina would expect us, of course, which made flying any closer far too dangerous.

As we crested the final hill and broke through the tree line, vast fields swept out for miles below us under a dark and brooding sky. Fitting for our general mood.

Small towns and rolling hills dotted the landscape, reminding me of the pictures I'd seen of Tuscany. The towns grew in size as they approached a towering, isolated hill with a relatively flat top and steep, almost vertical sides.

It was what covered the plateau that had me standing there gaping. If I thought seeing the fae's crystalline Summer Palace in the Otherworld was breathtaking, it had nothing on this.

The entire city was built around a colossal tree.

Blue-green leaves that reminded me too much of Jessa's angelic eyes fluttered wildly in the strong winds, but the behemoth-sized branches hardly moved. Like Venice, canals and rivers laced across the hilltop and below limbs, flowing beneath roots and carving their way through the city like streets. Only more extensive than the Italian city in every sense of the word.

Even though there were distinct structures, every building, every road, every bridge appeared to be all one giant, reddish-orange structure. Like they were molded together somehow. Maybe even grown from the rock itself.

The waterways flowed to the plateau's edges until they spilled over into roaring waterfalls. Rainbows danced in the air everywhere water fell.

Woven bird nests hung from the thickest branches, which stretched out past the cliff-like edges of the hilltop and toward the sky. The nests were large enough for a family of phoenixes to make their home. Some of the nests farther out on the branches swayed in the wind, with no ground beneath them for several hundred meters. Phoenixes in bird form flew everywhere, creating a flurry of activity no matter where I looked.

The part that truly took my breath away, though, was the palace.

Buildings spiraled their way upward around the trunk, ending at a nest-like structure in the first fork of branches. This fire-colored design was shaped more like a wide cup or bowl, giving it the appearance of having a deep rim. The scale of it all was hard to judge, but considering the birds looked like gnats from where we stood, the palace must have been several stories high and as wide as a football stadium.

My blood sang as if it knew it had come home.

Only then did I see the heads.

Even with my enhanced vision, I couldn't make out the details—thank Dazhbog—but the pikes on which they sat were unmistakable. Rising bile burned the back of my throat.

Tearing my gaze away, I looked down. Armies stretched across the fields, though staying back from the hilltop's steep sides and waterfalls. Phoenixes and griffins milled about as they set up camps and readied for the attack. Although the clouds were grey and menacing, no rain had fallen yet. I wasn't sure how long our luck would last.

I chewed on my bottom lip. There were so many more people here and ready to fight for freedom than I could have ever dreamed. There must have been thousands. And the city must also hold thousands, all under Galina's thrall. I knew they weren't all trained warriors, but I didn't doubt her magic would make them fight to the death with whatever they could get their hands, teeth, or talons on.

How many of those wondrous structures would be damaged in the attack? A worse thought: would we be enough to save all these people?

"Impressive, isn't it?" Pietr asked as he joined me. He handed me a bluish-green breakfast bar.

"The city or the army?" I took a small bite. My appetite was nonexistent, but I needed the energy.

Out of my periphery, I caught his faint smile. "I meant the army. But I suppose the city is as well. Or will be once you give it back to the people."

I couldn't agree more. My gaze returned to the structures at the tree's base. "What are the buildings made of? They seem to flow together."

"Fireglass," he said casually.

I furrowed my eyebrows and took another bite. "Never heard of it."

"It's a technique we learned from the *drakony*." He rested a hand on his sword hilt, likely a subconscious move as he eyed the city he'd once called home. "When the builders among us add our phoenix flame to the natural sand, it turns into a nearly indestructible building material."

Pavel's family might have helped build this magnificent city. I'd have to ask him. I swallowed my food and asked, "The dragons taught us that?"

"Their fire is very similar to our own, but they can only use it in full dragon form."

"Sounds like a con to being a dragon," I said.

Pietr smiled again, an expression he wore much more frequently than when I first arrived. "Yes, but they make up for it in other ways."

"Like what?" I finished off the breakfast bar.

"In bipedal form, their skin retains a shell-like coating which protects them from weapons of all kinds, including magic." He handed me a jug of water. "Not invincible, but close enough. And as dragons, our griffins look like mere chicks."

Yikes. I drank a few refreshing gulps and handed the jug back. "I suppose that makes up for only being able to breathe fire in one form."

He laughed and patted my shoulder. "Don't worry. They all but vanished a decade or two ago."

Someone called Pietr away, leaving me to ponder the dragons' disappearance in silence. Although, ever since my royal outing, silence didn't last for long.

A throat cleared behind me. I turned to find Ivan a few steps away. I waved him closer, a plan starting to materialize in my mind.

"Is everyone in the city under her spell?" I asked.

"As far as we know, yes," he said, his gaze sweeping across the landscape below us. "Even those in the surrounding villages."

I was afraid of that. "We need to get inside."

He chuckled. "Yep, that's the general idea."

I turned to face him directly. "No, I mean just you and me. Once I show the army proof of who I am, portal us in so I can confront her directly *before* the battle even starts. The fewer innocent people hurt, the better."

"That's the goal in any war, but casualties will happen." He didn't address my sneaking in plan.

"If I can take her down before the fight breaks out," I pushed, "then there won't be *any* casualties."

Considering that, he narrowed his green eyes. "Pietr will never go for it."

I shrugged. "Then we don't tell him."

"He's gonna be pissed." Ivan's grin was practically diabolical. He was in.

"He'll get over it." I returned my gaze to the battlefield below. "This is what a thief does. Only this time, it'll be a whole city that I steal."

By the time we made it across the fields and into the main camp, the hilltop that held Sokol had grown to immense proportions. The plateau was still some distance away, at least a half-mile if I had to guess.

Still, it became clear why Pietr had said only an aerial attack plan would do any good against Galina's spellbound army. Scaling those vertical cliff sides would take far too long and make us much too vulnerable to a counterattack.

Word spread that I arrived, and boy was I glad to have Pietr back at my side. Warriors came out in droves to cheer me on as I walked through the rows of tents. Boots and hooves had trampled most of the grass into the ground, and muddy footprints and cart tracks had already started to accumulate, thanks to the soil's moisture.

I still didn't know the first thing about being a leader, but I knew that these people needed hope. So, I raised my fist into the air, earning whoops of excitement. I felt absolutely ridiculous, but sometimes doing the right thing meant being uncomfortable. If the right thing were always simple, no one would choose otherwise.

I mean, *I* didn't always choose the right thing.

Pietr had sent some of our warriors ahead to set up camp within the middle of the amassing army. This time, he refused to let me pitch my tent. I wasn't sure if he was embarrassed for me or just trying to save time, but I was secretly grateful either way. No one needed to see that mess. Although, if my plan went off without a hitch, then the temporary shelter would be wholly unnecessary.

As we neared our collection of tents, a small group of warriors waited for us. Immediately, I recognized them: Feodora, Mila, and Taisiya. The rebellion's women leaders. Standing before me, they were even more fierce than in their incorporeal forms from the communication circle.

All three bowed before me.

"Your Majesty," Mila said in her deeper voice, her golden eyes almost translucent in person. "Welcome home."

"She's not home yet," Taisiya said, gesturing toward the colossal tree. "Not till that tyrant's head meets the end of my sword."

"We're not monsters," Feodora chided. "She will receive a fair trial. Likely to end in her execution, yes, but fair nonetheless."

"It better," the redhead grumbled.

I smiled. Only Ivan knew I'd already claimed Galina's death for myself. "Thank you. For fighting back, for not giving up, for being here. For everything."

A hush fell over the crowd. Angry muttering spread like wildfire, and I looked in the direction everyone else did. Three human-shaped figures rose over the plateau—two of the royal guard and their massive, multi-hued wings, and a more petite form between them who I could only assume was *her*. Galina.

I narrowed my eyes at the imposter. From this distance and with the guards flanking her, I couldn't tell if she had wings of her own. Actually, I *knew* she didn't. There was only one tsarina here, and that was me.

Calling my magic to me, I let my wings unfurl. My feathers weren't the thick plumes of the royal guard but instead were a golden, gossamer-like texture that shimmered in the sun. I wasn't sure if I had imagined this part when Zasha helped me accept my royal powers and inherit my ancestral memories. Turned out I hadn't.

The ground beneath me fell away as I rose. Warriors around me stood in shocked silence for only a moment before they burst into a chant. Over and over, they shouted my name—Veronica, tsarina of Mirfeniksa.

I continued to rise until I faced the usurper directly above the sea of men and women ready to die for me. They had no idea I had zero intention of letting them do so, but they cheered for me all the same, further driving my need to save them. I would do my damnedest to make sure they went home to their families unscathed.

Using my heightened falcon vision, I homed in on Galina's face, the woman who had stolen my life. Had stolen my family's lives and hundreds of others' lives as well.

A crown rested on her head, dark brown hair falling straight around her shoulders. Eyes a unique pinkish-purple hue stared back at me, venom in her otherwise pretty gaze.

That's right, bitch. I'm coming for you.

I took a deep breath and released my falcon screech. Only instead of letting it go wherever it pleased and potentially hurting my people, I focused it on her. The ripple of power from my ancestral awakening surged over everyone's heads and blasted against Galina and her guards.

The three of them nearly lost their balance in the air. Fear crossed Galina's face as one of the ropes holding her slipped, and she ended up almost sideways.

I smirked. The cables connecting her to the guards had been well hidden, but not enough for my avian vision when facing her directly. Now everyone would see through the charade.

She yelled something at the ground. A bolt of blueish-white magic streaked toward me, and I lurched to the side just in time. An icy burn grazed my arm. I lowered myself to the ground as Pietr yelled out commands to take cover.

War had begun, and William's mages were helping.

CHAPTER 27

Saturday Morning

Everything moved quickly after the mages' attack. Bolts of ice continued to blast around us, along with giant fireballs hurled from above. Dirt and debris flew into the air around the camp.

Those in charge barked out orders to their various units, and the warriors rushed to obey. As much as I'd wanted to get to Galina before anyone was injured or killed, the battle's chaos would provide excellent cover for my break-in. I'd have to do my best to minimize casualties now, which meant getting in as fast as possible.

I had no idea what Galina had promised William in exchange for his help, but I intended to find out with as little bloodshed as possible. Well, as little of *our* blood as possible. I'd spill all of theirs when I got a hold of them.

Pietr had given me back my knives before leaving Gavan, but the blades had been expertly cleaned. With paralyzing poison no longer an option, I would do my best to go for knockouts before kills with anyone else we encountered.

Since I already wore my armor and weapons, I moved straight to finding Ivan. Thankfully, I didn't have to look far. We made eye contact a few yards away, and he tilted his head toward a tent behind him—time to jump. I nodded and aimed for the tent.

Pietr fell into step beside me. "Why do I have a bad feeling about this meeting?"

"Because you think so poorly of thieves?" I grinned to let him know I was teasing.

He caught my arm, forcing me to stop just outside the tent. "Seriously, Veronica. What are you planning?"

I met his gaze straight on. "Ivan is going to get me inside the palace, and I'm going to kill Galina. The people she's controlling are innocent, mostly. I don't intend to let them kill their family and friends or die for her against their will."

He stared at me another moment before a small smile spread across his face.

That was not at all what I expected from him. "What?"

"Putting your people's interests before your own— you're thinking like a leader," he said.

I made a face at him and ducked inside the tent flap, Pietr still at my heels. "You're not stopping us."

He chuckled. "I don't intend to."

Ivan glanced up from where he was buckling on his sword belt. "You're coming with us?"

"No, but you need to take Pavel," Pietr said. "He's the best fighter among us."

I raised my eyebrow. "Better than Lena?"

He shook his head. "Lena's too emotionally involved and therefore too risky."

Ah. Her parents' death. He was absolutely right, but I was a bit shocked he was helping us this way. "I thought for sure you'd try to stop us."

His smile held a hint of sadness. "Your people have seen you alive and well and in your full glory. Now they have hope. If you can prevent them from killing their friends and family under Galina's spell, then they'll be loyal to you forever. I can't stop you—no matter the cost."

His last words hung heavy between us. He meant if we died in the fight. While I didn't intend to let that outcome happen either, our final deaths were a legitimate possibility.

If I needed to die to free my people, then so be it.

By the time Pietr brought Pavel to us, we were armed to the teeth and ready to go. The way Pavel looked us over meant Pietr hadn't told him what he volunteered for. More like volun*told*.

"We're sneaking in and killing Galina directly," I said. "You in?"

His dimples flashed with his grin. "Why, Veronica, I thought you'd never ask."

More than anything, I wanted to match his infectious grin, but the reality of what we were about to do caught up to me. I gripped the hilt of my sword. There was a good chance none of us would make it out alive. As long as we took Galina down with us, then it would be worth it.

No matter the cost.

"I have one more thing for you," Pietr said, drawing a gun from behind his back. He held it out toward me.

Perplexed, I took the weapon. It was a revolver, a six-shooter with a long, narrow barrel. I had seen a picture of this kind of gun long ago when studying weaponry with my dad. It was a Colt Single Action Army, and if the signs of age were any indication, it might've been original. As in from the late 1800s.

"How do you have this?" I asked, turning the gun over to inspect it.

"My family's had it for decades, acquiring it after some arrangement with a human peddler," he said. "I'm not sure it'll even fire anymore, but if anyone would know how to use it properly, it's you."

I opened the cylinder—one bullet. One would be all I needed, *if* the gun even fired.

"Thank you," I said, tucking the revolver safely away. I didn't want to tell him, but if I had to use it, chances were I'd already lost. "Keep them alive."

He nodded and met each of our gazes in turn. "May Mother Mokosh guide you home."

Like before, my skin prickled with the blessing. I wanted to take the time to thank him for everything he'd done for this realm, and for me. Teaching me what it truly meant to be a phoenix and to embrace my role here. To say a real goodbye, just in case. But doing so would mean further acknowledging the fact that we might not return, or he might fall in battle.

No, I would say a proper thanks once he joined me in the palace. That was the only outcome happening today.

Understanding filled Pietr's rainbow gaze, and he left us to finish our preparations without another word.

"Okay, here's the plan," Ivan said while Pavel added a few more weapons to his collection. He was an excellent swordsman but having other options never hurt. "I can get us into the city and close to the palace but not all the way inside."

"How do we get in?" I asked.

Ivan grinned. "It just so happens I was an apprentice to the royal blacksmith and learned a few things about the city's weaknesses. One of the waterways hides a series of complex tunnels for sewage and waste."

I crinkled my nose. "That sounds shitty."

"We don't have to swim, thank the gods, but the smell will be strong." Ivan handed us scarves to wrap around the bottom half of our face. "This'll help a little."

If I kept my eye on the prize—Galina's head on a platter with a side of battered William—I could handle anything. Even waltzing through shit.

Thunder boomed overhead, and a strong wind shook the tent. Or it could've been a spell landing far too close, which meant we needed to get the hell out of there.

"Once we get through the tunnels, there's only one way to go—up," Ivan continued. "We'll keep to the shadows and servants' stairs as much as we can, but we'll have to cross the *rotonda* in the open."

My eyebrows drew together. "What's that?"

"The equivalent of a throne room," he said. "It won't be occupied during the battle, but the tsarina's quarters are beyond it and inaccessible by any other route. Security precautions and all. If Galina's as self-absorbed as she seems, then that's where she will be."

Another boom of thunder rolled overhead, this time confirmed by raindrops tapping against the tent's fabric.

"We better go before the storm gets too bad," Pavel said, the drizzle already building to a steady beat. "The waterways are known to flood during heavy rains."

The three of us pulled our hoods over our heads, drenching the top half of our faces in shadows.

Ivan reached out and took our hands. "Ready?"

No. "Yes."

Pavel nodded, and the ground dropped out beneath us.

I squeezed my eyes shut, but the feeling that the world had suddenly lost all gravity remained. The good news was I didn't feel like my insides were being pulled apart and rearranged like they did when using the reapers' teleportation devices. Solid ground returned beneath my feet, and rain battered against my cloak.

I opened my eyes.

The palace was beyond breathtaking up close. Next to ivy-covered walls that reached dozens of feet upwards, we stood on a sort of narrow platform. Extensive waterfalls poured down from the rain, which drove its way through the upper branches and leafy canopy. An orangish-yellow tint came from within the glass walls and glittered with fiery red sparkles—fireglass in all its glory. The colorful patterns wove together, resembling a nest.

When I finally tore my gaze away from the dizzying sight above us, the rushing water of a canal only a few feet away caught my attention. A bridge spanned the canal just above our heads, and falcons of all sizes flew by, readying for battle or seeking cover from the storm. The deep blue leaves around us were thick enough to keep our movements hidden.

Damn, Ivan's realm hopping accuracy was on point.

Not having a fear of heights turned out to be a blessing because the canal dropped off the platform only a couple of steps behind us. A quick glance over proved it was a straight drop to the rest of the hilltop city below.

Without a word, Ivan motioned for us to follow. The platform and canal appeared to run parallel alongside the wall, curving around the palace's perimeter. An additional, subtle water flow joined the central channel through a screen of green ivy. With all the other blue and green plants draped across the walls, this entrance was virtually invisible.

We pushed our way through the hanging vines and into a dark tunnel. Even though we hadn't reached the sewers yet, my eyes watered, and my nostrils burned. I couldn't have been more thankful for the fabric covering my mouth and nose.

A footpath barely wide enough for two adult feet continued beside the waterway. Our steps made no noise. Each of us were well-trained in stealth and general sneakery. Even if we weren't so quiet, the rushing water would help hide our approach.

We twisted and turned, taking lefts and rights until I lost track of wherever the hell we were. My avian vision only helped me see the path, not keep my sense of direction.

Unlike the glass-like walls outside, rough stone blocks made up these inner tunnels. Water lines indicted the times it had flooded, and mold and moss crept along each mark. The palace must have been built with a rock foundation for some reason. Perhaps an original construction was covered over by fireglass once learning the method from the dragons. For all I knew, the entire city might have started out this way.

Ahead, a stream of water spilled down the stone wall, running across the walkway before splashing into the canal. Ivan hopped over the flow deftly, like he had done it a thousand times before. Just how many times had he used this entrance?

I'd rather have wet shoes than risk a slip, so I stepped into the water. Instantly, I realized my mistake. My foot slid out beneath me on the sleek path, likely from years of contact with running water. I toppled toward the water below, my arms windmilling in the air. I closed my eyes and readied for a wet and possibly feces-filled impact.

A hand caught mine and hauled me back onto the walkway.

Thank Dazhbog for Pavel's fast reflexes.

He winked at me, and I gave him a thankful grimace, my pulse still racing. As helpful as a layer of shit would be to keep enemies at bay, I *really* didn't want to deal with that level of disgust. I let out a slow breath before following Ivan once again.

We reached a sharp turn. The way Ivan paused and crouched down before the corner made me worry that we had gotten lost somehow.

"We're here," he whispered.

I peeked over his head. The waterway continued to flow down the tunnel, passing two guards on the left who stood beside a stone staircase leading into the belly of the palace. The way up was lit by sconces on the walls.

Two guards to take down, and we were in.

CHAPTER 28

Saturday Morning

I drew my sword and a knife, mentally preparing to take lives if I had to since I'd left the usual sedative option back in Miami. In theory, two guards should be a piece of cake for any of us, but we didn't know what kind of magic they'd be capable of in Galina's service.

Ivan bent to pick up a small, loose rock and threw it at the water in front of the guards. The stone landed with a splash. With their attention diverted, we made our move.

I rushed forward, Ivan taking one guard and me the other. I blocked a flash of steel with my sword and followed up with a jab from my knife. The grunt confirmed I'd gotten through a gap in the armor. I twisted around behind him and knocked him hard against the back of his head with my sword's pommel.

The guard staggered to his knees from the force of my hit. Pavel wrapped an arm around the man's neck in a chokehold until his eyes rolled up, and he slumped to the ground. Although I was sure he'd be out for long enough, we used his sword belt to bind his wrists to his ankles behind his back for good measure.

A deafening roar snagged my attention toward the waterway. The water level was rising quickly and churning with force.

"Ivan, hurry!" I yelled, leaping onto the steps leading up just as water sloshed onto the walkway. Pavel dragged the knocked-out guard behind us.

Ivan kicked the guard he fought hard in the chest, sending the man stumbling away from him. Ivan dashed for my outstretched hands. The ground rumbled, and a surge of water crashed through the tunnel, sweeping the guard off his feet and swallowing him whole.

I grabbed Ivan's hand, practically dragging him up the stairs behind Pavel. The flood chased us and lapped at our heels. We stopped running only when we reached the first landing, and the waters ceased to rise.

Pavel collapsed next to the guard he'd hauled up, who was still out and unaware of his near demise. His friend wasn't so fortunate.

"That must be one hell of a storm," I said, still panting.

Ivan wrung out the bottom of his cloak, forming a small pool at his feet. "The gods are making themselves heard."

I raised an eyebrow. "Did your bet tell you whether they're for or against us?"

He grinned. "Based on how much I won, I'd say for."

"Is that another bet?" I asked.

"Never press your luck."

I eyed the choppy water licking the top step before the landing. "Why the hell did so much water rush through there?"

"Engineers built this tunnel specifically to collect water during a storm," Ivan explained. "The natural force creates energy so we don't have to use our inner flames for mundane tasks all the time. Every tunnel up above flows through here."

I gave him an exasperated look. "That would've been nice to know beforehand."

"I did tell you it flooded," Pavel chimed in, climbing to his feet.

"*That* is not what I pictured." I gestured to the flooded tunnel.

Once we finished catching our breath and shook off the near-drowning—although I seemed to be the only one affected by that last part—we drew our weapons and crept up the stairs.

Flames danced in the sconces, sending shadows skittering along the walls and my nerves into overdrive. Every flicker and crackle made me think someone was coming, only to realize a second later it was just the lighting.

My pulse beat wildly in my ears with each step. I'd never been so annoyed at fire before in my life. Unlike most of my past jobs, this break-in came with some serious, definitely fatal consequences if we got caught. Not just for me, but for my friends and all the people fighting on my behalf.

The stairs continued to climb ever upward; the walls,

ceilings, and floor turning to reddish-orange glass after two levels. From time to time, brightly lit hallways led away from the stairwell, and voices echoed down the corridors. Other than two servants who wandered into our path and ended up incapacitated and tied up in a storeroom, we didn't encounter any more real obstacles. Everyone was focused on the war outside.

Maybe the gods really were on our side.

By the time we reached the rotonda, the battle had arrived at the palace. Falcon cries mixed with the clashing of steel and twang of arrows. Bursts and booms of magic crashed against the glass walls.

I gripped my weapons tighter. We were running out of time to save lives.

The rotonda's massively domed hall stretched out before us, columns sparkling with gold holding up the ceiling several stories above our heads. The room was empty, but we knew guards would be waiting on the other side, down a corridor leading to *her*.

Ivan crept forward out of the shadows that had helped hide our ascent. He paused with a hand on one of the columns and turned to look at Pavel and me. Smiling, he crossed his arms over his chest, fists to shoulders, then held them above his head in a V-shaped salute.

My instinct was to roll my eyes and wave him on, but this was it. We might not make it out of here alive, and he was ready to give his life so that I could win. So that a traitorous bitch would get what was coming to her. They both were. The least I could do was pay him the respect he so deserved.

I bowed my head.

When I looked up, he winked and turned. His dark cloak swirled around his legs as he bolted across the room. Pavel and I wasted no time rushing after him.

A high-pitched whistle was the only warning we had.

Bluish-white lightning struck the floor in front of us, spraying shards of ice in every direction.

I flung up my hand, stopping them from embedding in my face. My arm took the brunt of the attack, even through the vambraces. Gritting my teeth, I swiped my sword's blade across my arm to knock off as many as I could, blood dripping down my skin from where the ice pierced through the armor. I dove to the side as another bolt of frozen lightning streaked toward me.

"Did you think we wouldn't expect a thief to hide from the main fight?" William's voice called out.

The fae man strode out from a darkened recess. Silver-white hair hung straight, brushing against the dusky-grey skin of his long, thin neck. His eyes were such a light blue they resembled icicles, especially with the hatred that shone through.

Mages in robes and wielding staffs streamed into the circular room from the direction of Galina's suite, surrounding us and blocking the two exits.

"A reformed thief," I said. "And the true tsarina of Mirfeniksa."

His thin lip curled up. "So the rumors say."

I sensed Ivan and Pavel tense beside me, but I held up a hand to stop them. "You know they're more than rumors. Why else would Galina send someone to murder my brother and me?"

"Ah, yes. I suppose you must be right." William circled us, clasping his hands behind his back. "Unfortunately for us both, the queen is not very happy with me. You see, I was supposed to have drained you of your magic and killed you before entering this realm. I didn't expect you to follow."

I shrugged. "I'm not exactly predictable."

Ivan snort laughed beside me.

"Indeed not." William's gaze flicked Ivan's way then back to me. "I had hoped this one would be a suitable replacement. Sadly, no one can replace you. If only I'd known who you were at the stadium, I'd never have let you go."

As if he had a choice in the matter. But also, why the fuck was he stalling? "Are we really going to sling words all day, or are you ready to die?"

I didn't wait for an answer. I pushed magic into my blades and rushed him. Pavel and Ivan engaged the mages, knowing that they were mostly just magicians in ridiculous clothing—not exactly skilled fighters. Their only advantage was numbers.

William smirked as I closed in. He flicked his fingers toward me, and ice blossomed beneath my feet, jerking me to a stop as it gripped me in place. I heated the ground beneath me, freeing myself within a heartbeat.

He drew a long knife and tapped the handle. Fire danced along the blade—phoenix fire. All around me, the mages' staffs lit up with matching flames.

Well, shit. That wasn't good.

"You can thank your new friend for letting us siphon his magic," he said and struck.

Our blades connected over my head, sparks flying around us. Meeting his gaze for a split second, I noticed an odd glow to his pupils that hadn't been there before. I jabbed at him with my knife. The steel swept through nothing but air, and I staggered forward at the sudden loss of pressure against my blade.

A chilling chuckle rolled around the hall, sweeping across my skin and scalp, raising the hairs all over my body.

For fucks' sake. *Bill* was the realm walker?

No wonder he was able to move about so easily. I knew the ability manifested randomly in any species, but I'd never heard of the fae having it. If more Winter Court fae had that gift, then the human world was in serious trouble.

"Come on out, coward." I turned in a slow circle, my blades held loose in my hands to taunt him further.

Pavel and Ivan fought back-to-back, fending off spells and sweeping aside staff swings. Sweat dripped down both their faces, their expressions locked in grimaces. This needed to end soon.

"As you wish," the coward drawled.

Blue lightning streaked toward me again. I spun on my heel, twirling out of the way and letting the ice crash to the floor. The waves of ice kept coming, each strike more erratic than the last as I continued to avoid them.

Pavel let out an anguished yell, and I whipped around to look. He was on his knees, a fiery staff pierced through his chest. He gripped it in his hands, his face a mask of pain and agony. Time slowed to a stop.

No.

My breath caught in my throat, and I stepped toward him, forgetting everything else. A spell crashed against my back, icy tendrils slithering around my body and locking me in place. My armor kept most of the cold magic from touching my skin, but where the ice bit through, it hurt like a motherfucker.

Just not as much as my heart did.

I hissed through my teeth, tears freezing against my cheeks. William finally came out of hiding, his steps sure and purposeful as he approached me. In my periphery, two mages held Ivan's arms while a third leveled a blazing knife at his heart.

"Ah, the little bird has been caught at last," William said, his blue eyes as cold as the ice binding me. "You've been an annoying thorn in my side for far too long. With my trap in the forest, I was this close to bringing Galina your head. It has been truly infuriating that someone as simple as you has been able to interrupt my plans."

He chuckled, a dark and hair-raising sound. "Never again."

My lips were frozen shut, effectively paralyzing and silencing me. Which was a shame because I had a *lot* to say right now, though mostly with my blades.

"Did you not wonder how Galina managed to seize control?" he asked. "How she drove your parents from this land?"

I channeled my hatred through my gaze.

He chuckled again, circling me as he did before. "I'm sure you did. The answer is simple: she's not a phoenix."

That didn't make any sense. She launched the coup that drove my parents out of this world. Why would anyone follow her if she wasn't a phoenix?

What the fuck was she then?

"I can tell you're surprised," he continued, "but don't feel like too much of a fool. She deceived everyone, including your beloved angels. Well, everyone except me."

Gods, he was so fucking arrogant.

He stopped in front of me, a crazed gleam in his eyes. "You must be wondering what I get out of this arrangement."

I didn't actually care. I just wanted to stab his eyes out. He stepped closer anyway, reaching up to tuck a loose strand of my hair behind my ear. His touch made me want to vomit.

"Once we crush this little rebellion of yours, Galina will claim me as her mate, and I will be the *tsar* of this realm." His hand moved to my throat, applying enough pressure to make his point. "Then we'll take the others—yours and mine. I am of the *Béar* clan. No one will be able to stop us. Not the Summer Court queen. Not even the angels."

A chill that had nothing to do with his magical hold ran through me. I believed him. I'd seen the results of his necromancy in person, fought against undead hordes that he had created.

Not only that, but in addition to their seasonally named courts, the fae also organized themselves into clans based on an animalistic hierarchy. Only a Lion of the Summer Court or a Bear of the Winter court had enough power to seize the throne.

And Galina? With whatever magic she possessed, she had managed to control the people of Sokol, somehow convincing them she was a phoenix and the rightful tsarina. Was she a witch as strong as Kit? Another one of the fae?

Or something else altogether?

Smiling, William released my throat and stepped back. "I'll do you the honor of letting you watch your two friends die today before I kill you. You'll have to take my word that the agent and witch and all the others you've foolishly befriended will die slow, torturous deaths."

Rage built within me, writhing and rising into an insatiable need to kill. There was no sin or shame associated with this desire—this man deserved to die, needed to die to save the Community and the people of my realm. I would deal with any guilty feelings that came up when all was said and done.

Time to show him who the fuck he was dealing with.

CHAPTER 29

Saturday Morning

I met William's gaze straight on. I knew from his faltering smile that he saw his death shining from my eyes.

Good.

Unleashing my fury, I let it pour through my limbs, through every fiber of my core. A need for justice raced through my veins until it was all that I was. The magic that rose from within was not just my own, not entirely. It was raw. Feral. Mixed with the memories of my mother and my ancestors, the tsarinas of the past going back millennia. All their power joined me at once, and all of us were fucking pissed.

Wings forged from the gods themselves broke through the ice binding me, unfurling from my back in a blaze of heat. As the flames rose, the remaining ice holding me shattered, flying in all directions and clattering to the ground.

Fire licked the air hungrily, seeking more to quench its voracious thirst.

William took a step back, raising an arm to ward off the fire's sudden warmth. Behind me, steel and wood clattered to the floor, and footsteps scurried backward.

With speed I didn't know I had, I hurled my knife at the mage threatening Ivan. From the mage's shout, I had distracted him from making his killing strike against my friend. I gripped my sword in two hands, and flames fueled by my rage rushed down the steel.

My turn.

I attacked William relentlessly. He struggled to fend off my swings, and I kept coming. I was past caring about defending myself, but he never got a good hit in any way. Strike after strike, I attacked, and he deflected.

After a bone-shattering blow from me, he stumbled to his knees. I stood over him, anger and anguish surging through me in undulating waves. I raised my sword for the last time.

His eyes widened. "Wait—"

I swung hard, the fiery steel slicing through the necromancer's neck with ease. I let his body and head topple to the side, forever captured wide-eyed and open-mouthed. He would have to take his words with him to whatever fae hell existed.

I turned to face the other mages.

Some turned to flee, only to find their way barred by my wall of fire. The remaining mages attacked with staffs and spells.

I cast aside the physical hits one after the other while absorbing their magic full-on. The power of my ancestors still coursed through my veins, burning away anything they threw my way. I was done playing games. This was *my* world.

Spinning and chopping, I took them down one by one until every one of them was dead or simply defeated. Not a single mage stood to challenge me further.

My chest rose and fell hard. Blood ran down my sword's edge, dripping to the floor. I glanced at the doors leading to Galina.

I wasn't done yet.

"Veronica," Ivan's anguished voice shattered my rage. He knelt beside Pavel, who lay on the ground, his breaths raspy and shallow.

Grief a writhing monster within me, I strode toward them, igniting a circle of fire around us to keep any newcomers from doing anything stupid. Collapsing on Pavel's other side, I took his hand in mine, holding it to my cheek. "I'm so sorry."

His lips struggled to form a smile. "Don't be, moya koroleva. I would die for you any day." He grimaced. "Go... take back your throne... find... your mate."

His eyes glazed over, and his chest ceased to rise again.

I bowed my head, letting the tears slide down my cheeks. Very few people actually deserved to die, and Pavel was not one of them by a long shot. I would hold his cheeky grin and love of the human world in my memories forever to honor him.

After setting his hand gently on his stomach, I unbuckled my cloak and laid it over him. "Rest now, my friend."

There was one more person I needed to kill, and she was waiting for me just beyond the next set of doors. Gritting my teeth, I rose to my feet.

"I'll protect him," Ivan said, his magic entwining with mine as he took over the flaming circle protecting us. "Bring us home, V."

My wings billowed out behind me as I stepped through the fire. I pushed open the double doors leading into the tsarina's chambers, striding into the room like I owned the place. Because I did.

Four guards stood at attention in the corners of the elaborate room, their eyes blackened like the hunters in the forest. In the middle of all the luxury stood Galina.

The woman who took everything I loved away from me was beautiful. Inhumanly so. Dark brown hair fell in loose curls around her face, and her eyes held a pinkish-purple hue, a color I hadn't seen before today. Her skin was pale, but not in an unhealthy way. Instead, it seemed to glitter with a silver coating. I had no idea if it was makeup or natural.

She wasn't a human mage; that much was obvious. Whatever ability I had that allowed me to sense otherness about Community members whispered around me like a living entity. She was more powerful than most I'd encountered before, but I still had no idea what she was except about to die.

After all the magic I'd used today, there wasn't much of my inner flame left. What I did have wriggled inside of me, desperate to be let out to take back what was mine. I obliged.

A fiery strand of magic whipped toward her from my outstretched hand, encircling her neck and tightening. Claiming her to surrender.

Instinctively, she reached up to grasp at the snare, only to pull her hands away with a gasp. Smoke drifted off her palms. The guards surged forward, but she raised a hand, and they stopped mid-step. Not out of loyalty—magic.

What kind of sorcery did this woman yield? And how? Gods, I wished Kit was with me now.

"I always had a sneaking suspicion Jackson lied." Her voice was deep and sultry, and a faint crackle of magic laced her words.

A slithering sensation crawled through my mind. I burned her out.

"Your magic isn't going to work on me," I said, tightening the hold on her neck until she winced. "What are you?"

She tilted her head to the side, a curious expression crossing her face. "I thought you would have figured that out by now."

Ugh. I hated this game already—time to move it along.

"Whatever," I said. "I'm taking back what's rightfully mine."

The woman had the audacity to smile. "Rightfully says whom?"

"Oh, I don't know, history, people, gods." Clashing of steel and thunderous booms resounded outside the balcony doors behind Galina. Too many were dying.

"The time for ascension purely based on lineage is over," she said calmly. "Humans, the lowest of sentient creatures, taught us to value ingenuity over genetics."

"Whether that's true or not doesn't matter," I said. "This is a checkmate type of situation, and you've lost. I order you to release Mirognya from your magic."

"Oh, I don't think so." The black of her pupils leaked past her irises, filling the whites. It bled into the veins of her cheeks and down her throat. When it reached my magic encircling her neck, the fire snuffed out, black ashes fluttering in the air between us.

Oh, fuck.

Like flicking a light switch, darkness enveloped me in its smothering embrace. Winds whirled around me, whipping me about. I stumbled as I fought against the sudden drafts.

Before I had a chance to wonder where the hell I was or if I had even gone anywhere, a sword appeared from the encircling shadows. Agony ripped through my thigh, the blade slicing through my leather pants as if they were little more than butter. I turned to face the attacker, only to find the sword gone.

I held my sword in clammy hands, clenching my teeth against the pain. Again and again, blades flew by, slashing at every part of me. There was no way to tell where the next attack would come from. There was nobody to watch for tells, their muscles predicting their next move. My skin grew cool as blood collected and dripped from too many places to count.

As suddenly as it started, the darkness vanished. I blinked at the sudden bright light. I was back in the palace, if I had left to begin with.

Galina stood precisely where she'd been before, her hands clasped in front of her. "Have you had enough?"

I faced her, drained and bleeding, my sword hanging loose from my hand. My inner flame had shriveled to a tiny pinprick of light. Despite all the time I'd spent training with Pavel, I was out of magic.

My lungs constricted with fresh grief. I wouldn't fail him. I couldn't.

She laughed, somehow knowing exactly what was happening. "Oh, you poor child. Just as ignorant as your mother."

"You think you've won." A statement, not a question. Alas, she wasn't smart enough to recognize the difference.

"I know so. You have nothing left, and I still have all of this." She waved a hand toward me, and her magic followed.

Once again, the shadows enveloped me in a menacing hold, ready to swallow me whole as soon as she gave the word. My hair, sticky from blood and sweat, slapped against my neck and cheeks as the swirling darkness closed in.

It was now or never.

I sent a prayer up to the gods and drew the revolver. Through the darkness, I raised the gun, pulled back the hammer, and squeezed the trigger. The last bullet exploded from the barrel.

Time must have slowed down. I watched the shell roar through the dark magic and cross the distance between us. Ripples in the shadowy air followed in its wake.

Galina's eyes opened wide before the bullet split the middle of her forehead, lodging itself firmly in her skull. Her body collapsed to the floor.

I might not have known what she was, but no creature could withstand a direct shot to the brain.

Ingenuity over genetics.

The four guards took a step toward me, only to pause and shake their heads. Confusion crossed their faces, and the whites of their eyes returned. Her magic was dissipating.

I dropped the revolver and strode to the balcony doors, wrenching them open. As I approached the fireglass parapet, the sounds of battle swept over me, along with driving rain. Fierce winds tugged at my armor and hair. I gripped the edge of the low wall, blood washing down my arms.

Far below, muddy battles had broken out across the fields leading toward the city's cliffs. Thick smoke billowed into the air all over Sokol and burned my nostrils. Archers armed with flaming arrows—phoenix fire, no doubt— loosed death into the crowds below. Falcons and griffins screamed as they clashed together in the air, talons and beaks raking against each other. Feathers fluttered everywhere I looked.

No more death today.

I reached inward, asking my withered flame to give just a little more. We didn't need much, but we still had a job to do. We had to stop the carnage.

By the grace of the gods, we found the strength.

Fiery wings spread from my back once again, and I rose into the air. My wings beat steadily against the winds. I needed to get their attention—*everyone's* attention. I aimed for a spot above the cliff face, where both armies could see me clearly.

The rebels recognized me first, their attacks faltering as hope filled their faces. The other side didn't understand what was happening, so I decided to help them out. I set myself on fire, raised my sword above my head, and let loose a screech.

This wasn't just any screech, but a battle cry full of raw power—that of the royal bloodline. Proving beyond a shadow of doubt to those she had held enthralled that I was who I claimed to be.

Across the fields and camps below to the upper branches far above, Galina's army stuttered to a stop. They ducked instinctively as the force of my call swept over them all, breaking the final tendrils of her hold at last.

Overhead, grey clouds pulled apart, and a single beam of sunlight tumbled from the sky to illuminate me in all its glory.

The gods approved.

It was over.

CHAPTER 30

Saturday Morning

I returned to the balcony, rushing back in to find Ivan. My fiery wings dissipated into the air as sparks and ash. The guards who had been protecting Galina followed me without question, and I let them. Based on the grimly determined looks on their faces, they would spend the rest of their lives proving their loyalty to me.

Ivan still knelt beside Pavel, the circle of flames gone, as were the mages.

I turned to the guards. "Search the palace for any remaining humans and fae. They need to pay for their crimes as the others did."

With luck, William would be the only realm walker among them, and he was dead.

Three guards immediately followed my order, calling out commands as they ran into the corridors outside the rotonda. One stayed behind, and I didn't argue. Protecting me was their job as well.

I knelt beside Ivan, placing a hand on his shoulder. As much as I wanted to stay and mourn with him, there were still those alive who needed us. "Let's go save your family."

Intense grief dulled the usually bright green of his eyes. "He's my best friend, and he's gone."

"We will give him the send-off he deserves," I said gently. "But your family may still be alive, and Pavel would want you to be reunited."

He let out a deep sigh and nodded. His gaze snagged on my face. "You're a bloody mess. Pavel would think you look so hot right now."

The surprising comment made me smile. "So true. Pavel will always be with us."

We stood and headed for the door, the guard on our heels.

"What's your name?" I asked the grim-faced man.

His eyes widened, making the turquoise color pop. Maybe Galina never bothered to ask. "Vladimir, Your Majesty."

"Can you lead us to the dungeons, Vladimir?"

"Of course, moya koroleva." He bowed and stepped in front of us to lead the way.

As we descended, anyone we encountered proved far more afraid of us than we were wary of them. They cowered in corners or ran from us completely, and I assumed that this was the typical reaction for anyone coming out from beneath

Galina's spell. Guards were trained to get right back into the game, no matter the enemy or threat.

To be honest, I was glad we didn't have to fight anyone else or explain who I was or have a conversation at all. Even with all the training over the past two weeks, I felt sluggish. Beyond exhausted after the magic I'd used.

By the time we reached the lower palace levels that made up the dungeons, my legs were quivering beneath me. But I refused to break. I wanted to see this through to the end.

I needed to.

We'd left the fireglass's beauty several levels up and encountered nothing but dingy and moldy stone blocks the rest of the way. I didn't know whether it was like this all the time or only under Galina's reign, but I would make it a point to have these older walls and floors scrubbed clean.

Everything would be different from now on.

Vladimir commanded the jailor to open the prison's outer door, a wooden beast of an opening with metal brackets and a bar lock. Keys clattered together in the jailor's shaking hands, but he managed to slide the right key in on the first try. The massive door opened into darkness before us.

The stench hit me first. My eyes watered with the sting even as I tucked my nose into my elbow. Wails and cries came next, sending chills up my spine with their anguished tunes. Sconces along the walls flared to life, revealing a hallway and a row of cells on either side.

Ivan rushed forward, glancing inside each cell until he stopped. He gripped the bars, grimacing as steam rose from his palms. The metal had been treated with magic, but he didn't let go.

"Mama," he called out, his voice breaking.

"Ivan?" The woman's voice was hoarse from little use and lack of water.

"Open them all," I commanded, forcing myself to lower my arm from my nose. These poor souls had lived in this reek for Dazhbog knows how long. I could manage it for now.

Vladimir hesitated. "Your Majesty, some of these feniksy are actual criminals. I wouldn't—"

"As of this moment, everyone starts over." I raised my voice to be heard above the din. The cell's occupants hushed others to hear. "Whatever crimes were committed under Galina's rule are forgiven. Any crimes that occur the moment these doors open will be punished. Understood?"

The jailor gulped but fumbled for his keys again. As he opened each cell, I walked down the corridor, telling the prisoners who I was and what had occurred today. A few remained in their cells, either too weak to move or not trusting what I said as truth. I asked Vladimir to send people down to help them once we finished.

One or two bolted for the door without a second glance, but the majority reached out to touch me as I passed, whispering blessings through their tears.

For the first time since I discovered who I was, I felt like I had actually earned praise. Not in a boastful, egotistical sort of way. At least I hoped not.

By simply being me, I had given my people enough hope to fight against a tyrant and live free. Seeing her up close and knowing what she had done to this land, I finally understood why the people of Gavan wanted to show me their respect.

I returned to the cell Ivan entered. He rocked a frail woman in his arms, shushing her gently as she cried. Another more petite figure embraced him from behind, twig-like arms doing their best to wrap around his middle. I wanted to join them, to scoop them up and take their pain away. This was their moment to share.

As I backed away quietly, the figure behind Ivan glanced up. A girl, most likely his sister, if her bright green eyes were any indication. Recognition flashed to life in her bold gaze, and she mouthed the words *thank you.*

I smiled and left Ivan to his family.

I told Pietr that I wouldn't consider planning a coronation until all the dead were gathered and given a proper send-off as they returned to the sun. He fought with me in the beginning but eventually backed off when I threatened to run away.

Hey, I had no issues with bribery and threats to get my way.

Those who had been under Galina's spell held hollow, empty gazes as they helped clean up the damaged city and return home. Time would tell if their guilt faded, and I would do my best to show them what a fair ruler looked like. No magic necessary. I certainly didn't blame them for their actions while spellbound.

From what we could determine, Galina had somehow mixed phoenix fire with dark shadow magic to hold them all against their will. How she had managed to do it, or how she had learned it was possible in the first place, was still a mystery. The phoenixes she drained in the process had taken any answers with them to the sun.

May they rest in peace.

It took almost two days, but by Monday afternoon, the rebel army and some new additions had cleared the fields of battle debris and made room for the dead. I worked right alongside them. The rain had stopped after my fiery display above the city, but the ground was still covered in thick mud and pools of blood. We were all covered in both by the time we finished, but no one complained.

Billowing white smoke rose into the air from the funeral pyres, a fitting tradition for those born of the flame. I watched the tendrils dissipate into the sky and meld into the scattering of pink and purple clouds, hoping those souls had found their eternal peace. Sunset had come far too fast, and the death toll weighed heavy on my shoulders.

Hundreds had died true deaths, including Pavel, and each one because of me. Because I found my way back to Mirognya and discovered the truth of my heritage. If I hadn't been so fucking impulsive to follow a diabolical fae necromancer through an unknown portal, all of them would still be alive. Enslaved, maybe, but alive.

An arm slung around my shoulders, beaded dreadlocks tinkling with the movement. Lena. I smiled and leaned into her.

"It's not your fault," she said.

I gave her a shrewd look. "What, are you a mind reader now?"

She snorted. "Anyone with eyes can see you're blaming yourself, but Galina did this. Not you."

"I'm sure I'll believe that someday." I took a deep breath, the smoke strong inside my nose and filling my lungs. "Just not today."

"To think, your parents kept you from this world, hoping to save you from her, and ended up turning you into the impulsive, griffin-headed phoenix that could bring a tyrant down." She danced away from my punch. "I think they'd be proud of you."

I rolled my eyes. "Only after they punished my disobedience for a few decades."

"Eh, you deserve it." Her playful grin reminded me so much of Pavel that it hurt, but she turned her gaze back to the fires before she saw the evidence.

I really did think my parents would be proud of me, even if it was my death-provoking ways that got me into this current mess. In the end, I had done it—I had found Maddox's killer and brought her to justice.

I would finally be able to sleep at night.

CHAPTER 31

Friday Morning

I was used to living life in the fast lane, but in the days following the funerals, even I felt like I was in some dizzying funhouse trying to catch my balance. Plans for my coronation took off, turning the palace into a flower-filled festival. Apparently, phoenixes were *really* into flowers, not that I was complaining.

I tried to stay out of the way as often as possible, but after Pietr dragged me into decor discussions for the third time, I appointed him captain of the guard. Poof: he suddenly had more important things to do. My relief was short-lived, however, because Liz stepped in to take his place. At least she was kinder about my lack of attention span.

The main problem was, I couldn't stop thinking about Miami. About *home*. For a short while, I felt like Mirfeniksa had become home, and maybe it would be someday. But right now, home meant Thane, no matter how fleeting. I needed to tell him everything that had been weighing on my heart, everything I should have said weeks ago, if only to get it off my chest and live without regret.

"If you wiggle one more time, I'm going to stab you with this needle." Liz waved the tiny weapon in my face. She was sewing me into my coronation dress.

Today was the day.

I laughed. "Okay, okay. Fair enough."

She resumed adjusting the dress's fit. "Where'd you go this time?"

"Thane," I sighed.

Over the last week, I'd given the twins all the details about my unfortunate, cosmic-level connection with the reaper.

"You'll see him soon," she murmured.

"Every day that passes makes me more anxious," I said. "I know it's more than likely that he's already ascended, but I can't shake the feeling that this mark still being here means he hasn't. What if I miss my chance?"

"If the gods saw fit to throw a grim reaper and a phoenix together, then they'll make sure it happens." She cut the thread with her teeth. "There."

I looked at myself in the mirror and smiled. Fancy dresses weren't in my closet's rotation often. I usually reserved them for occasions like Star Island masquerade parties, where I had random first encounters with my flame's mate. Shying away from girly looks wasn't on purpose; it just came with the job. I held the skirts out and twirled in a circle, enjoying the way I felt in this gorgeous lilac dress.

It was a plunging V-neck look with long, nearly translucent billowy sleeves. Though thankfully still hiding my bonded mark. I wasn't ready to show that bad boy off to everyone just yet. The organza gown cinched at my natural waist before flowing into an A-line skirt that split up my right leg.

Embroidered golden flowers and crystals decorated the top half and trailed off over my hips. If I wore this in the human world, I would've felt a bit like an overstuffed peacock on her wedding day.

Mirfeniksa had changed me for the better in the few short weeks I'd been here. Being so close to bringing Kit here to experience it herself—with Angela, of course—lifted my spirits into a don't-give-a-fuck level. If Liz wanted me to strut like a peacock, then that's exactly what I'd do, with all the pride I could muster.

She fluffed my blonde hair around my shoulders, letting the loose curls settle comfortably yet fashionably. Then she reached over to a box someone brought in earlier. Lifting the lid revealed a golden crown. It was much more ornate than the one she'd gotten me to wear before, with gemstones that perfectly matched my dress.

And here I thought the dress color was to match my eyes.

I bent at the knees so she could place the crown on my head. The weight of it wasn't uncomfortable, but I was definitely aware of the change.

"Isn't it going to fall off?" I asked.

"Only if you try to do a cartwheel or something." Liz chuckled and looked me over one more time. "Ready?"

I smiled at her in the mirror. "Not really, but I suppose I'm a better choice than Galina, right?"

She shook her head at me like the lost cause that I was. "That's the spirit."

An hour later, I paced the length of the waiting room. Evidently, a priestess needed to announce all the so-called important guests—as in those with titles—and allow them to take a seat before the actual ceremony could begin. Had I known that earlier, I would've waited in my damn room and taken a nap.

The only self-important guest not here was Adrik, and I would deal with him and his lack of attendance in the battle as soon as possible. I ground my teeth together. He better have a good fucking reason for flaking out on us, like being dead.

The door opened, and I halted midstride, hoping this was my moment. I wasn't sure how much longer my nerves could last. In strode Pietr. I sighed. Not that I wasn't glad to see him, but it meant they still weren't ready.

Just how many dignitaries were there?

Pietr chuckled. "Not a fan of waiting, I take it?"

"Is anyone?" I asked.

"Good point." He gestured toward the padded bench I hadn't used yet. "Sit. Let me tell you a story."

I sat, careful to lay the skirt out to avoid wrinkles.

He leaned a shoulder against the wall, one hand resting comfortably on his sword's hilt. "When I was a young child, my parents took me to see the griffins for the first time. I'd seen them in passing, of course, but it's not nearly as exciting seeing one bogged down with harnesses and goods to carry as it is seeing them free to roam and fly as they please.

"Most of the domestic griffin population is kept at *Tsitadel*, the Stronghold. Long ago, our people built Tsitadel into the cliffside of the *Vechnyy* mountain range. It's accessible only by flying, but the height allows the griffins to come and go as they pleased.

"They're not pets, as you recall." He winked at me. "But keepers do train them to return and follow commands using a positive reward system. Praise and fish go a long way to keeping them happy, as does a vigorous cleaning routine. Those big beasts love getting scrubbed."

The image of a griffin sudsed up in a bathtub nearly did me in.

He continued, "Now I hadn't mastered shifting and flying in falcon form by that age, which meant we would have to get into the hold by griffinback. Even before we arrived, I could see the animals fall from the cliffside, catch the breeze, and swoop away. It was exhilarating beyond words, even for a lad who'd often seen his parents come and go with wings." He smiled. "At the base of the mountain is an outpost, hardly used as such anymore, but it has a robust history from the *drakon* wars."

"Dragon wars? Why didn't I learn about any of that yet?" All I'd been studying was modern-day politics and a who's who guide. So boring.

He held up a hand. "All in good time. This is a story about griffins, remember?"

I sighed and waved him on.

"The outpost also holds stables and corrals for unicorn training," he said.

"Wait, I thought you said unicorns were difficult to catch."

"Difficult but not impossible. And once caught, they're fiercely loyal." He crossed his arms. "Any more interruptions?"

I clasped my hands in my lap and smiled innocently up at him, lips pressed together.

"The outpost is also where you purchase a flight to Tsitadel," he said. "We're waiting in line when I noticed one of the unicorns in a nearby corral. This one was a majestic beast, a coat so black it almost looked purple and a silver horn like starlight. He was rearing back and whinnying whenever anyone dared approach him.

"At the time, I didn't understand what was happening. I watched the unicorn's eyes roll with fear as the men surrounded him with ropes and knew I had to do something to stop them. I let go of my mother's hand and ran over, easily slipping between the fence slats. I ran right up to the unicorn, turned around, and put my hands up to stop the handlers."

My eyes widened. "Holy shit. Your poor mom."

Pietr grinned. "Oh yes, I was quite the troublemaker as a child."

"Still are by rebel standards," I pointed out.

He laughed. "Fair."

"So, what happened?" I asked.

"As luck would have it, one of the griffins saw me run over. Griffins are incredibly protective of their young and, thanks to our longstanding symbiotic relationship, also of phoenix young. Just as the unicorn reared back, ready to stomp me into oblivion, the griffin charged in. She took me under her wing and screeched at the unicorn, which quickly and wisely corrected the direction of its stomp and bowed in submission. From then on, the handlers used griffins to help tame the unicorns."

I waited for more, but that was the end of the story. I blinked at him. "While enjoyable, what's the point of your story?"

"That sometimes, being impatient can be just as important as patient." He pushed himself off the wall. "And now, it's time to go."

"Was this just a distraction?" I asked, already knowing the answer.

He winked. "Of course."

I laughed and followed him toward the door. His plan had undoubtedly worked.

Hesitating before turning the knob, he turned and took my hands, kissing my knuckles. "If you believe nothing else, know that you were born to be a queen. It doesn't matter how you were raised or how little time you've had to adjust. It's in your blood."

My cheeks heated with his praise. "Thank you. For the pep talk *and* the distraction."

"My pleasure, moya koroleva." He squeezed my hands before releasing them and ushered me out the door.

How I had been so blessed to call this man my friend, I'll never know. Especially considering that night in Gavan's hot spring. Maybe things would have been more awkward if he'd seen me around Thane, kind of like how Colin had acted. I had a sneaking suspicion Pietr would handle that situation just as respectfully as he did now.

Besides, I was sure Taisiya would make sure he wouldn't be lonely for long.

A few steps later, I entered the grand hall. If I hadn't been clenching my teeth so tightly together, I would have gasped.

As with the rest of the palace, golden-red fireglass made up the arched ceiling, which rose several stories and added to the overall vastness of the hall. Breezes blew in from the open windows at the top, cooling the interior. Falcons of all shapes and sizes perched around the windows and along crossbeams. Below them, phoenixes in human form occupied every pew-like bench.

Had the entire phoenix population of Sokol gathered?

Not even close, of course, but when hundreds of faces—both humanoid and avian—turned to face me at once, shit got real. The cacophony of noise stuttered to a stop, replaced by murmurs, whispers, and fluttering feathers.

A deep violet aisle runner spilled between the bench rows, leading to the base of a raised dais. The gathering of priests and priestesses waited for me there.

This was it.

Taking a deep breath, I let my wings of fire unfurl, the immediate warmth at my back soothing my nerves. Gasps and excited cries rang out, along with a few chirps from the rafters above. I began the long walk down the aisle.

If my life of secrecy were any indication, I wasn't a huge fan of the spotlight. Keeping my teeth clenched together, I nodded at random people as I passed, avoiding smiles because I'd probably end up looking like a madwoman. Maybe I was a bit, considering *I* was somehow becoming the equivalent of a queen.

Madwoman or not, I made it to the dais and lifted the edge of my dress to ascend the few steps. Eight priests and priestesses formed a half-circle on the platform, surrounding a throne in the center—*my* throne.

Was this real life?

The religious leaders wore long flowing robes, each in a different color and buttoned closed at the shoulders. The high priestess, Annika, stepped forward.

Long and straight, her greyish purple hair matched her similarly colored irises. A unique combination, mainly because the grey wasn't from age. Her skin was flawless. She was slightly taller than me but more of a Kardashian sister in the curves department. She bowed to me before facing the gathered crowd, smiling.

Her voice rang out clear and strong, "Rejoice, for our tsarina has risen again."

The crowd went wild, cheering and throwing flowers and hats up into the air. Falcons along the rafters fluttered their wings and screeched. I smiled. I couldn't help it. Their exuberance was contagious.

When Annika regained their attention once again, the ceremony began in earnest. Each clergy member came forward to give me their blessing, as well as our gods' and goddesses' blessings.

I must have blacked out at some point because the next thing I knew, the high priestess ushered me toward the throne. I sat, my gaze falling across the crowded room. More than one phoenix let the tears fall freely or wiped at their noses with a tissue.

"Long live Her Majesty, Veronica Mirilla Neill," the priestess's voice rang out, "Tsarina of Mirfeniksa."

It was done. I was a motherfucking queen.

EPILOGUE

Thane

I had become very familiar with Kit's apartment over the last month. It was where we met to discuss anything we discovered, to follow new leads on the internet, or to simply commiserate.

Her girlfriend, Angela, might not have known Veronica well, but her empathy provided us both with relief in the form of comfort food—for Kit, anyway—and hugs. I wasn't usually a fan of hugs, but Angela had a way of drawing you in like a mother hen. Maybe it was the big brown eyes.

I teleported into the hallway outside the apartment door, tucked the cylindrical t-port device into my pocket, and knocked. After the unfortunate event involving two naked bodies on the couch, Kit banned me from ever teleporting straight into her home. She'd lifted the ban shortly after with a request to call or text first. I continued to arrive outside anyway as an added precaution.

The door opened, and Angela's sprite-like face greeted me. Besides her eyes, the only things large about her were her curly brown hair and personality. She smiled and stepped back. "Happy ascension day, Thane. Come on in."

The one-bedroom apartment was an open concept, providing a complete view of everything from the kitchen on the left into the living room straight ahead. Despite the money she made as Veronica's partner in crime—not to mention the family money—Kit preferred minimalism.

Well, except when it came to her body art and piercings.

The brief thought of Veronica shot a pang through my heart, and as had become more common, the red mark on my chest burned. I rubbed at it. Knowing it would be gone with my impending ascension, I hadn't bothered to ask anyone about it.

Kit strolled out of the bathroom on the right, pulling her multitude of beaded braids into a ponytail and displaying the shaved half of her head. Her eyes were the same dark brown as her hair, her skin only a few shades lighter. Today she wore a black blazer over a t-shirt and jeans, the sleeves rolled up to display the striped pattern beneath. It was the fanciest outfit she'd ever worn around me.

Angela moved to stand beside Kit. Besides their shared shorter stature—even if Kit was still a few inches taller—they were as opposite as two people could be. I was glad that I would still be able to work with them in my new role at the Death Enforcement Agency.

"You ready?" Kit asked, her gaze seeming to penetrate my soul.

I knew she meant more than just physically. "I'm not sure I'll ever be ready, but my time is up."

Angela chewed on her bottom lip, and her eyes were already bright with tears. I needed to get out of here soon. I withdrew an envelope from my back pocket and handed it to Kit. She glanced at Veronica's name on the front then back up at me, confused.

"Just in case I change my mind about giving it to her as an angel," I said. "She may never return, but if she does, I want her to have it. I may not have that same desire when I have wings and a severe lack of emotions."

She nodded and tucked the envelope into her blazer's inner pocket.

I cleared my throat. "Thank you both for assisting in the search. I know you and V are as close as sisters. I'm sorry we failed."

"Trust me when I say that stubborn phoenix will find a way home." Kit said.

I smirked, knowing all too well what she meant. Nothing stopped Veronica when she put her mind to it. "I'll see you both after the ceremony."

Angela smiled. "We'll be there."

I activated my teleportation device and stepped into the black circle, letting the world fall away for the last time.

I love to get to know my readers. You can reach me on Facebook, Instagram, or Twitter **@stephaniemirro**. Sign up for my mailing list to get new release information, special deals, giveaways, become a part of my ARC team, and more. I look forward to hearing from you!

www.stephaniemirro.com

Veronica's story continues in…

WINGS

OF

LIFE

THE LAST PHOENIX: BOOK FIVE

Coming this fall.

GLOSSARY

Adam Larue – Archangel of Miami

Adrik – phoenix; rebel leader

Albert Renauldo, Dr. – human plastic surgeon; owns Star Island mansion

Annika – phoenix; high priestess

Anthony "Tony" – piano shop owner; friend of Veronica

Broderick Ó Faoláin – fae duke; *deceased*

Colin Ó Broin – Autumn Court fae

Death Enforcement Agency – also known as the DEA; agency of the human world that keeps the Community safe

Drystan Neill – father of Veronica; *deceased*

El Sombra Mercado – also known as the Shadow Market

Enrique Alvarez – human street musician

Feodora – phoenix; rebel leader
Frank Turner – human mage; ex-necromancer
Galina Volkov – unknown species; false tsarina
Giovanni "Joe" Facchini – fae regular of The Morning Grind; friend of Veronica
Isaac Davidson – human manager of The Morning Grind; boss of Veronica
Ivan – phoenix; rebel
Jackson Reed – realm walker; in prison
Jessa – angel; healer
Katherine "Kit" Parker – natural born witch; best friend of Veronica
Katya – phoenix; birdkeeper
Lizabeta "Liz" – phoenix; healer
Luciana Pérez – natural born witch; owner of The Witch's Brew shop in *el Sombra Mercado*
Luka Navarro – alpha of the Miami werewolf pack
Maddox "Mad" Neill – brother of Veronica; *deceased*
Mama Anya – phoenix; midwife
Manuel – owner of food truck in *el Sombra Mercado*
Mila – phoenix; rebel leader
Nathan – angel; fighter
Officer Harris – receptionist at prison; species unknown but most likely a troll
Oleg – phoenix; rebel fire communicator
Owen Cooper, Dr. – head mortician and grim reaper at the DEA
Papa Boris – phoenix
Pavel – phoenix; rebel
Pietr – phoenix; rebel leader
Rhiannon Neill – mother of Veronica; *deceased*

Rogelio Diaz – natural born warlock; deep in his cup somewhere

Sophia Clark – grim reaper agent of the DEA

Tabitha Delgado – werewolf

Taisiya – phoenix; rebel leader

Thane Munro – grim reaper agent of the DEA

The Morning Grind – a DC-based coffee shop in Miami; Veronica's day job

Veronica "V" Neill – the last phoenix

Viktor – phoenix; rebel spy

Vladimir – phoenix; palace guard

William Caomhánach – Winter Court fae and unseelie

Xavier Garcia – Master Vampire of Miami

Yelena "Lena" – phoenix; rebel

Yury – phoenix; rebel scout

Zasha – phoenix; Veronica's aunt

ACKNOWLEDGEMENTS

My entire family has been so supportive of my writing career, but I need to give a special shout-out to my husband, Tim, and my mother-in-law, Linda. Without them, none of this would be possible.

But the thanks don't end there!

To my editor, Melissa Simmons; and my beta readers, Marty, Tom, Kimmie, Jessica, Michelle, Alisha, Rachel, Lauren, Devon, and Erica, *thank you.*

To Claire Holt of Luminescence Covers, who continues to amaze me with these covers, *thank you.*

To all my friends and fans, who showed their support in so many ways, *thank you.*

There's nothing cooler than knowing people enjoy what I write.

ABOUT THE
AUTHOR

Stephanie Mirro's lifetime love of ancient mythology led to her majoring in the Classics in college, which wasn't quite as much fun as writing her own mythology stories as she did growing up. But that education, combined with an overactive imagination, being an active fantasy reader, and having a vampire obsession, resulted in a writing career.

Born and raised in Southern Arizona, Stephanie now resides in Northern Virginia with her husband, two kids, and two furbabies. This thing called "seasons" is still magical.